SCULPT A MURDER

ALSO BY LILY ASHTON

PAINT A MURDER

Sculpt a Murder

Lily Ashton

Lily Ashton

An *Alice Haydon* Mystery

Published by Magenta Lily Publishing 2019
London, Great Britain

ISBN 978-1-9161062-2-2

Cover design by Design for Writers

Chapter 1

It was strange but true, that once Alice Haydon had secured her dream job of senior art curator, she quit.

The post at Gregory's House Art Gallery had been a good one. Alice was delighted that after eight years her efforts to climb the greasy corporate pole had led her to the top curating job. But having got there, she decided that she would prefer to work for herself. Fed up taking direction from bosses who did not have her interests at heart, she figured that striking out on her own would give her the creative independence she craved. And she had landed a big contract straightaway. A high-profile project with a prominent local family.

Her long legs took Alice through Renton Hall's stone-flagged porch and into the warm welcome of her new client. Eleanor Carberry's sunshine smile brightened her leathered face. A long white dress hung off narrow shoulders, a daisy-embroidered sash hugged her waist. She wore a gold crown.

"You must be Titania," said Alice. "That's a lovely outfit."

Alice introduced Eleanor to her boyfriend Joe.

"It's a grand place you have here." Joe Buchanan raised his soft Irish voice over the laughter of a boisterous group behind him. "And I like that you're having a bit of a shindig before you lay the new carpets."

"Now that the structural work is finished, the decorators want to get cracking." Eleanor tucked strands of fine hair behind her ears. "So we decided to have our annual Midsummer Night's party before they start. It's three weeks late – I do hope people won't think we're completely bonkers."

Alice shuffled closer to Eleanor. "I'm sure they won't, they'll be too interested in seeing what you've done with the place. Converting a family home to a boutique hotel is quite an undertaking."

"So we've discovered! It wasn't an easy decision and we'll have to get used to strangers staying in our home. But we're determined to make it a success." Eleanor threw her arms in the air. "But now we party. And you look lovely, Alice. Have you come as Hermia?"

"No, I'm just a general fairy." Alice held out the skirt of her pink dress. "And it's not every day I get to say that!"

"Evening Eleanor." A stooped man lifted his trilby hat as he went by. "Always a pleasure to attend a party at the Hall." He limped into the house, thumping his walking stick into the floor with each step.

"That's Bill, our neighbour," said Eleanor. "He always walks around to the front door and his wife, Elsa, uses the shortcut to the back. She's probably here already."

"If I had a choice between the long way and the shortcut," said Alice. "I know which I'd pick."

"Enjoy the party. There are drinks and food in the conservatory. And Alice – do show Joe around. I'm sure he'd like to see what you're doing for us here."

Alice took Joe into the library, where empty bookshelves lined the walls. "The plan is to rearrange this room so there are less books, ironically for a library. But there'll be a bigger sitting area, especially around the fireplace."

"With a real fire, it'll be snug. I can see the reasoning."

They edged their way through chattering guests in the oak-panelled hallway, to the conservatory at the back of the house. An oval table groaned with food – pink and lilac macaroons and strawberries dipped in chocolate. A white-frosted cake decorated with pink rose petals was encircled by flickering tea lights in coloured glass jars.

Alice elbowed Joe. "What do you think of the ceiling decorations? It took us ages to fix them up."

Orange and black paper butterflies hung from the pitched glass ceiling, strings of white flowers fluttering between them. Alice bit into a teddy bear-shaped sandwich. The room would be perfect for themed events and parties at the hotel.

"Good evening, Alice," said a muscular man in a short green jacket over a bare chest. He wore a heavy crown with high arches. "Good to see you."

"Oberon, I presume? You look amazing."

"One does one's best," he said with a broad grin. "As this is the last time we'll have a big family party here, we thought we'd really go to town."

"Joe, this is Nick Carberry, Eleanor's brother and co-owner of Renton Hall."

"Alice told me you're a photographer, Joe. You should see some of the old family photos we've got stored in the attic." Nick put an empty glass on the table. "I told Eleanor that we should hang some of them around the place. I think the hotel guests would like to see the house's history."

"I understand your grandfather developed his own photos. That was an art in itself in those days."

"It was, but thank God for digital cameras, eh?"

Joe laughed. "Too true."

"This house is going to make a fabulous hotel," said Alice. "You must be so excited. Or perhaps you're nervous?"

"A bit of both." Nick grinned. "It's a wrench giving up the house; it's our family home after all and we've had some wonderful times here. But since Father passed away, neither Eleanor nor I can afford to keep it and we couldn't bear to sell it. We'll run the hotel together, though, so we'll still get to spend a lot of time here."

Alice's father had abandoned the family when she was six years old, so she did not share the Carberrys' happy childhood memories. In her bleaker moments, she had often imagined herself in a house like Renton Hall, surrounded by a large family and Labradors, building a trunkful of happy stories. No wonder Nick and Eleanor didn't want to let all that go.

"I see you've had the sculpture installed, Nick." Alice indicated a life-sized marble statue of a male figure with no face, on the edge of the decking. "Though I thought it was supposed to be on the other side of the lake?"

"I put it here tonight so that people can see it. It'll be moved tomorrow. What do you think of it?"

"I like it. It's striking and definitely a talking point."

"Well, that makes two fans. You and Eleanor's dog, who's developed a strange attachment to it."

"Ah, there you are Nick," said a silken voice. A tall, dusky woman wearing a saffron wraparound dress glided to Nick's side. Nick beamed and put his arm around her whittled waist.

"Alice, Joe – let me introduce you to Devi, my lovely girlfriend." Gold flecks sparkled in Nick's hazel eyes.

Alice's mouth dropped. "Oh my God, you're Devi Dutta. You were in *The Sunny Girl*! I loved that film and you were wonderful. Gosh, I can't believe I'm talking to a real Bollywood star." Alice knew she was gushing, but she didn't care.

"Thank you, I'm glad you liked the movie." Devi tossed back long, shiny locks and flashed a megawatt smile. "I loved making it."

Alice was entranced. She had only recently watched the film with her friend, Livvie Manners. The pair had sat on Alice's sofa, snacking on brownies from Livvie's café, watching the gorgeous Devi sashay across the screen. And here was the luminous star herself, right in front of her.

"I may be a tad biased, but I agree," said Nick. "You *were* fantastic, Devi. In fact I think it's your best performance yet. I can't wait to see your next film. It's scheduled for autumn, right?"

"The world premiere is in Mumbai in November, though it won't be in cinemas over here until early next year."

"What brings you to England, Devi?" said Joe. "Are they shooting Bollywood movies in England now?"

"No, I have a break from filming so I'm working on some of my other interests. And I'm here to see Nick, of course."

A solid man with thinning blond hair patted Nick's arm and whispered in his ear. Nick stiffened and dropped his arm from Devi's waist. He looked at the ground until the man finished speaking.

"Would you excuse me?" he said. "I have to deal with something. I'll be back in a minute."

Alice wanted to show Joe the rest of the house, so she led him up the dark oak staircase to the newly fitted bedrooms and en-suite bathrooms. They stepped over paint-speckled, creaky boards and peered out of naked windows to the house's grounds below. The empty walls looked sad and grubby. But tomorrow work would begin to transform the building's bare bones into a beautiful, luxurious hotel. Alice could not wait.

Back downstairs, they went through the conservatory and onto the deck. Two chefs in full whites with tall puffy hats moved hunks of meat on a smoking barbeque.

"Hello Alice," said a squat man with ruddy cheeks. "Glad you could make it."

"Harry. Isn't it the perfect evening for a midsummer party?"

"As always! Even the weather does the Carberrys' bidding." Alice noticed the edge of bitterness in his voice. Harry held out a hand to Joe. "We haven't been properly introduced. I'm Harry. Nick and Eleanor's cousin."

Joe took Harry's hand. "You must have seen a good few parties here over the years."

"I have indeed. I spent much of my childhood here, especially in the summer holidays. The Carberrys did a lot of entertaining then and there was always something exciting going on." He glanced up at the house and sighed. "Those were the days."

"I suppose with Mr Carberry's passing there was nobody to live in the house."

"Aunt Mary is still with us. But the house is too big for an old lady on her own, so she's moved to Scotland to be with her sister. Her family are from the Borders originally, so she's going back home really."

"And Renton Hall becomes Renton Hotel," said Alice. "In such a beautiful, peaceful spot, it's sure to do well."

"I don't doubt it'll be successful with Nick and Eleanor running it – and your beautiful curation of course. Though I hope that statue won't scare the guests away. It looks like something out of *Star Wars*."

Eleanor joined the group. "It's a good job you're standing over here, I think the catering staff are getting a bit carried away at the barbeque. I don't know why Nick insisted on having it."

"Because we all love it," said Harry. "The barbeque is always popular. Remember the one Nick did last summer? He must have barbequed a whole cow!"

"We did get through buckets of food, though I think Great Wheaton cricket team had a lot to do with that. By the way Harry, where's Cheryl? I haven't seen her."

"She snuck in the back and went upstairs to change. Now you mention it, I haven't seen her since."

Eleanor headed off to check on the bar. Alice left Joe talking to Harry and walked to the edge of the decking. Moonbeams shimmered across an inky lake, fading into the dark fields beyond. A wooden humpback bridge, sparkling with coloured lights, straddled the lake as it thinned into a stream. A couple hunched over the railing, watching the water.

Alice turned around and looked back at the house. Little points of flamelight bounced off the ivy leaves on the facade. Working on this project was a brilliant start to her new career. She really could not have hoped for a more thrilling job.

"Help!" It was a woman's voice, full of alarm and urgency. "Help!"

Alice spun around to see a figure thundering out of the gloom. She ran across the bridge, stumbled onto the decking and pulled up beside Harry.

"It's Nick ..." The woman's knees gave way as she struggled for breath. "He's dead."

Chapter 2

Harry grabbed the woman's elbow, hauling her from her knees and onto her feet.

"What are you talking about?" he yelled, shaking her arm.

The woman started to speak, but the words were choked in her sobs. She pointed behind her. "There," she said. Yanking her elbow from Harry's clasp, she ran back where she had come from.

Nobody moved.

"Shouldn't we find out what's happened?" Alice looked after the woman as she was sucked into the darkness beyond the bridge.

"I wouldn't worry," said Harry. "It's probably Nick's idea of a party piece."

Eleanor appeared on the decking, her crown askew. She grabbed Harry's arm. "I heard Cheryl shouting. What's going on?"

"Nothing, I should think. She's just making a scene as usual."

"I thought I heard her say that Nick was dead?"

"She did, but I assumed it was part of the entertainment."

"Don't be ridiculous." Eleanor paled beneath her crown. "Harry ..."

His expression changed instantly. "I'll check," he said, and ran into the darkness, breaking into a sprint as he crossed the bridge.

Alice had caught Harry and Eleanor's conversation. She watched Harry disappear before she stepped towards the lake.

Joe caught her arm. "Where do you think you're going?"

Alice glared over her shoulder. "To see if my client's still alive."

Alice jogged over the bridge and onto a path that ran straight ahead, a field on one side and a wooded area on the other. She hiked up her long dress and made for an outbuilding ahead, partly illuminated by a light fixed high up on the stonework. Joe caught her up and they passed the outbuilding together. They veered to the right and along a second path into the woods. Just ahead, Harry and Eleanor were crouched down, their heads together.

Alice slowed to a walk, but even before she reached it, she could make out the spreadeagled body of a king. By the time she reached for Joe's hand, she had already seen Nick Carberry's face. Alice looked away.

"Oh Nick. Nick!" Eleanor wailed as she knelt beside her brother.

A man rushed passed Alice to Eleanor's side. He put his hand on Eleanor's back as he bent over the body, then he turned to the little group of guests who had followed.

"Okay everyone, nothing to see." Tom tapped Harry's shoulder. "We need to clear this area."

"Okay, you stay with Eleanor," said Harry. "I'll take care of the guests."

Tom knelt beside his wife. She seemed to be tugging her brother's hand, as though urging him to get up. Harry stretched out his arms and shooed the guests out of the wood. Joe put his arm around Alice's shoulder, manoeuving her through the crowd and back to the house.

Guests who had been waiting for news rushed to greet them. One man with baggy trousers and a hat in the shape of a donkey's head ran over the bridge. "Is Nick really dead?"

Joe stepped in front of Alice before she could answer. "I think someone should call the police."

"Already have," said Bottom. "They should be here any minute."

Anxious whispers passed amongst the visitors. The chefs continued to turn steaks, but there were no more takers. As Alice walked towards the conservatory, two policemen burst through the doors and onto the decking. One ran ahead and straight up the path.

Inside the conservatory, DI Nathan Salisbury was talking to a woman in a waitress's uniform. Before she reached thc detective, Alice stopped and brushed her hands down the front of her dress.

"Hello Alice," said the voice of calm. "I'm sorry to see you in these circumstances. We happened to be close by when the call came through, so at least we haven't kept you all waiting."

The last time her path had crossed with Nathan's, they had both been following the trail of a murderer and art thief. Nathan had been the lead detective on the case, but Alice had pursued her own path to find the culprit. Alice had got there first.

"I don't know how such a terrible thing could have happened," she said. "Everyone seemed to be having such a good time."

"That's what I'm here to find out," said Nathan. "I'll go and check out the scene now. There are more officers in the hallway, so give them your details before you leave, please. And Alice, we'll need a statement from you at some point."

"You think I should go? I was wondering whether Eleanor would like me to stay and help. Clear up or something."

Joe put a hand on her shoulder. "We should go, Alice. Let the police do their job."

Nick Carberry's lifeless face kept popping into Alice's head as she drove home. Her client was dead and she had barely started her work at Renton Hall. But why? The blond-haired man who had whispered in Nick's ear had forced him to excuse himself. Who was that man? And what had he said to Nick? It must have been important, or Nick would not have left so abruptly. Perhaps it was a message to meet somebody in the woods. Maybe the blond man had killed Nick Carberry. So many questions, Alice was starting to feel giddy.

Alice parked her Defender in the underground car park of Joe's apartment block. Alice felt the need for caffeine and bounded up the stairs ahead of him. To remove Nick Carberry's face from her mind, she pictured herself pouring roasted beans into the grinder. She could almost smell the coffee.

She reached the top floor and was just about to switch on the light when she saw a tall, wiry man, his back towards her, leaning against Joe's front door. Alice held her breath. She pulled her fingers into fists and let her head sink into her shoulders. There was no sign of Joe behind her, so she raised her right foot to step back into the stairwell. Too late. The man spun around.

His eyes locked on hers. He smiled a toothy smile.

"Hello, Ally Pally."

Chapter 3

THE NEXT MORNING, ALICE lay in bed mulling over the previous evening's events. What had started as a happy family party to mark the beginning of a new chapter in their lives, had ended in tragedy.

Alice had met Nick Carberry at Renton Hall only the week before. The Carberry family had a large art collection and Eleanor and Nick had hired Alice to catalogue everything and select a few pieces to hang in the hotel. Nick had been charming and Alice was deeply impressed at how the pair had thrown themselves so passionately into the project. But what would happen to it now? Perhaps Eleanor would put the project on hold.

Alice got out of bed and rummaged through clothes on a chair. She pulled on a pair of tracksuit trousers and one of Joe's t-shirts. In the mirror she was horrified to see a messy mop of dark hair and lashes still caked in the previous night's mascara. Stumbling into the kitchen, she made straight for the coffee machine.

"And she's up! You never were good in the mornings were you, Ally?"

Alice said nothing. She made herself a mug of strong

coffee, sat down at the kitchen table and contemplated her brother. Green eyes peered out of a thin, oval face below short, dark hair in a polished quiff.

"You must have been up since the crack of dawn, fussing over that hair."

"Well it's better than the haystack on your head. You'd need a pitchfork to get through that."

"I don't have the money to spend on expensive hair products. Are you still getting your hair gel from San Francisco?"

"Well, I don't—"

"Easy, easy." Joe removed bacon from a frying pan. "I appreciate you haven't seen each other in a while, but I'm finding the kindergarten banter a bit much with my Sunday breakfast." He put a plate in front of each sibling. "Christian, you were no eggs, right?"

Christian nodded, picked up a fork and dived into his food. Alice glared at the top of her brother's expensively coiffed hair until she could resist the scrambled eggs no more. They finished their breakfast in silence. Afterwards, Alice curled up on the sofa as Christian explained why he had landed on her doorstep in the middle of the night.

"So, it wasn't until I got home late on Thursday that I found a bunch of suitcases sitting in the hall. Jasmine had gone on a business trip, but she left a note saying that she'd packed up all my stuff and I should leave immediately."

"I'm sorry it turned out like that, Christian. Though you can't have been surprised, she's asked you to move out, what, three times?"

"I know, I know. But I didn't think she actually meant it."

"Not even when she told you the relationship was over."

Christian closed his eyes, hugging his cheeks with his hands. Alice reached out and cupped his elbow. Was he going to cry?

"I'm not going to cry if that's what you were thinking."

"I wasn't." Alice swallowed hard. "But thanks for the heads up."

It had been six months since Alice had last seen Christian. She and Joe had stopped off in Manchester on their way home from a weekend in Glasgow. She liked Jasmine, but she could see that her ruthless ambition did not match Christian's easygoing attitude to work and life. Sooner or later, it would be an issue between them.

"So, what now?" said Alice. "You'll have to find somewhere to live presumably?"

"I can stay with friends for a bit while I look for a house share. Somewhere closer to the centre this time."

"Have you thought of buying a property? Surely you earn enough to get something half decent?"

"I'm not sure I'm grown-up enough for a mortgage!"

"You're killing me Christian. You're thirty-two."

Christian rubbed his stubbly chin. "It's not about the number, Alice. Besides, how would I afford all those expensive hair products on top of a mortgage?"

"Very funny. Seriously, where will you stay while you sort out something permanent?"

"Here! My boss has given me a couple of weeks' leave to sort myself out, so I thought I'd stay with you." Christian looked around the apartment. "Though I didn't realise you'd moved in with Joe. Some guy next door to your barge told me you were living here now."

"You've been to *Daisy Dawn*?"

"Naturally. The barge is – was – your home, Ally. The guy said you still rent it."

"That was Roddy Rafferty. Yes, I moved in here with Joe, but I kept *Daisy* on as an office. Now that I'm freelancing I need somewhere to work and I didn't want to clog up Joe's apartment with more of my stuff. Plus, I still like the idea of leaving home to go to work."

"I'm not surprised you kept the barge, it must be fun living on a boat. I wouldn't mind having a go myself."

Alice could take a hint. "Why don't you stay on *Daisy*? It would give you some space and I'll see you during the day while I'm working. Plus, it would take our kindergarten chatter out of the grown-up's apartment!"

Alice helped Christian re-pack and they loaded his bags into the Defender for the short drive to the river.

The barge was part of a small river-dwelling community that had been on the River Nare in Great Wheaton for over a century. *Daisy*'s owners had lovingly refurbished the barge, intending to spend their holidays meandering along Britain's waterways, until a lucrative contract had taken them overseas. So, they had rented *Daisy* to Alice. It was a turn of fate that had been Alice's salvation when she was looking for an affordable property.

"Wow, this is something." Christian circled the deck. "Talk about being close to nature. Look – a pair of swans are coming over to say hello."

"Jeez, Christian! Such excitement!"

"Well, I've never been on a barge before. Actually, I can't remember the last time I was even on a boat."

Alice unlocked *Daisy*'s hatch door and made her way down the companionway, dragging one of Christian's suitcases behind her. She went through the saloon and into her spacious cabin in the bow. Christian struggled after her, dumped holdalls and a backpack on the floor and rushed to the window.

"God, I'm going to love living here."

"Living? I thought you said you were just staying a couple of weeks."

"I've been thinking about extending my stay. My boss is being so understanding about my break-up." Christian flitted to the wardrobe, opened both doors, closed them. He pulled out drawers and stepped in and out of the en-suite bathroom.

"Knock, knock." A familiar voice came from the galley. "Can I come in?"

"We're in the cabin," said Alice.

A man with a scraggly beard and baggy tartan shorts appeared in the doorway. "Ah ha! Two Haydons in a room." He grinned.

"Roddy, you met my brother Christian last night."

"I did indeed. I hope you found Joe's apartment without too much trouble, Christian?"

"The taxi driver knew exactly where it was, thanks. Your barge, Roddy, is it the same as Alice's?"

"My boat is a bit more … lived-in than Alice's." Roddy twirled a strand of grey beard. "Otherwise, it's more or less the same."

"Don't listen to him, his boat is nothing like *Daisy*. Though it's not without its own charm. Now, I'll just show you where things are, Christian, and you can get yourself settled."

The men followed Alice into the saloon, and she pointed out power sockets and light switches.

"It's alright, Ally. I can work out where everything is."

"You can always ask me if you can't find something," said Roddy.

"Thanks," said Alice. "Christian, my friend Livvie runs *The Coffee Pot*, just along Sam's Way, the path by the river. She does great food, especially cakes. You'll probably end up getting most of your meals from there, like I do."

"I can attest to Livvie's wonderful cakes. And so can my stomach!"

Alice picked up a pink folder from the coffee table and tucked it under her arm.

"Not working on a Sunday are you?" said Roddy.

"I'm just going to pop over to Renton Hall to check in on Eleanor after last night. I'll take these photos back with me."

"What happened last night?"

Alice told Roddy about Nick Carberry's demise. "How a perfectly healthy man in his forties was suddenly dead in the woods," she said, "is a mystery."

"Dear girl, I do hope you aren't getting yourself embroiled in another investigation," said Roddy. "I'm not sure my nerves can take it."

"Another investigation?"

"Why don't you come over to my place, Christian? I'll tell you all about it over a bottle of red."

Renton Hall's front door was wide open. Alice peered inside and called Eleanor's name, but there was no response. She crept inside. Hastily abandoned drinks lay on the bare floorboards in the entrance area. In the conservatory, fairy cakes sagged and ruby juice from wrinkled strawberries, leaked over the table and onto the floor. It looked like the morning after Miss Haversham's hen party.

"Morning, Alice."

Alice spun around to find Harry Horton in the doorway. He was dressed in smart grey trousers and a Ralph Lauren polo shirt, but his chin spouted bristles and his eyes were swollen.

"I'm so sorry." Alice linked her hands. "I didn't mean to disturb you, but I wanted to ..." *Find out how your cousin died!*

"Give your condolences to Eleanor? That's thoughtful of you. Eleanor's at home with Tom and the children. It's been a dreadful shock for her. For us all of course."

Alice followed Harry's glance through the open doors towards the lake. A line of police tape ran from the bridge, along the paddock and to the outbuilding at the top of the path that had led to a dead body. A uniformed policeman was leading a line of people with bowed heads, as they inched their way across the field.

"They're looking for clues," said Harry covering his eyes with his hand for a moment. "No luck yet."

Alice put her hands in her shorts pockets and hunched her shoulders. For the second time that morning, she was dealing with a man on the verge of tears. Just as she was about to comment on the cloudless sky, DI Nathan Salisbury arrived.

"Good morning, Miss Haydon. Are you here to help with the search?"

"Er, yes, if that's what you want me to do."

"I'll leave you to it." Harry backed away. "I'm going to organise some lunch for everyone."

The last time Alice had worked on a case with Nathan Salisbury, it had been personal. Alice had seen a dead body in the river outside the art gallery where she worked. On top of that, a prize drawing had been stolen from the gallery, the central piece of an exhibition she was organising. Her reputation had been at stake and she had felt compelled to hunt down the offender.

But this time, she was not going to get involved. She realised it would sound callous, but she needed to know how Nick Carberry's death was going to affect things. Her job, specifically. She had bills to pay after all.

"Good to see you again, Alice." Nathan spoke more quietly. He moved his athletic body closer, a warm smile on his handsome face.

"You too, Nathan. Though I'm sorry it's because of that." Alice nodded to the searchers outside. "What are they looking for?"

"At this stage, anything. We don't know how Mr Carberry died and we need some clues."

"It was so sudden. But what was he doing out there in the woods in the dark?"

"Good question. And when we answer that, we may well know who killed him."

"What? I thought … How did he die?"

"Nick Carberry was killed from a single gunshot to the chest. He was murdered."

Chapter 4

A BLAZING SUN THREW shafts of light between the lush leaves overhead as Alice drove out of Great Wheaton. Christian fiddled with the radio as Alice contemplated her Tuesday morning. Assuming that Eleanor would put the decorating project on hold, at the very least, after her brother's death, Alice had spent Monday catching up with Christian. But Eleanor had called the previous evening and asked Alice to start work at Renton Hall the next morning.

Alice's plan was to sort through the Carberry's collection of paintings first. She needed to find out what was there and how many pieces would be useable in the hotel. But after Nick Carberry's murder, she imagined the house and grounds would be chaotic. Filled with police officers, and ghoulish rubberneckers wanting a glimpse of a murder scene.

She could not have been more wrong. Calm and serenity enveloped Renton Hall as the Haydon siblings entered the house. There was no evidence of Saturday's midsummer party – the ground floor rooms were clean and empty. Eleanor Carberry was sitting in a deckchair at the edge of the lake. A Yorkshire terrier, yellow ribbon tied around a topknot on its head, sprung up, surveying Alice with wary eyes. Eleanor turned around. She looked drawn and pale, her wan smile petering out before it reached her eyes.

"Alice, you're here. And you've brought an assistant."

Christian gave a listless wave.

"Oh no, this is Christian, my brother. He's staying with me at the moment, so I brought him along to see if he could help. It's just for today."

The dog barked as Christian stepped forward to shake Eleanor's hand.

"Shut up, Wilson," said Eleanor. "Ignore him, he just likes to make his presence felt." She stroked the dog's back. "Thank you for coming, Christian. I think Alice will need all the help she can get. Jeremy, our gardener, told me he's found more paintings in his snug. I didn't even know they were there. I'm not sure how you'll whittle down your selection from such a big collection."

"Don't worry, I'll find a way to sort them. I just need to collect everything together and assess what you have."

A pair of heels clicked on the decking and Devi joined them. The actress's face was drawn and sallow, and there were deep shadows under her eyes. Her hair was in a ponytail, and even without make-up she was hauntingly beautiful. She carried a canvas bag, which she eased to the ground to the sound of clinking glass.

"Oh my God, Devi Dutta!" Christian bounded over to the actress. "I just *love* your movies. I've seen them all. You're incredible!" He took her hand, pulled it to his lips and kissed it.

Alice crossed her arms and looked at the ground.

"Devi, you don't have to do that," said Eleanor. "Susan will take care of the empty bottles."

"I know, but I can't sit around watching everybody else working. I want to do something useful."

"Here, let me help you." Christian picked up the bag. "Where do you want it?"

Devi took Christian in the direction of the recycling area at the side of the house.

"Will you come with me to Jeremy's snug please, Alice? Let's see what he's found."

Eleanor took Alice's arm and the two women headed over the bridge, the stream bubbling beneath them. They walked along the edge of the paddock, the grass now flattened where the volunteers had scoured for clues. On the other side of the path, the wood ran in a near straight line.

"My father told me that his father, that's my grandfather Wilfred, used to take him through the woods and make him name every tree and plant." Eleanor pulled her mouth into a half moon. "Fortunately, Nick and I were spared that ordeal! Though we always knew how lucky we were to have our own wood."

"I haven't had a chance to say, Eleanor. I'm so sorry for your loss."

"I cried all day yesterday for my darling brother. But Nick would be furious if I didn't open the hotel on time. So, we carry on."

In the daylight, the brick outbuilding was smaller than Alice remembered. And she had missed its carved pale blue wooden doors. Stone steps at the far end led to a platform surrounded by a thin wooden railing.

"This was a dairy and hayloft once upon a time, until my father cut down the herd and planted more wheat. Now Jeremy uses it to store his equipment, but part of the space is a sitting area where he spends his breaks. Nick and I used to visit him a lot, so we've always thought of the building as Jeremy's snug."

They climbed the steps to the loft, which held odd pieces of furniture instead of hay. A tall, broad-shouldered man was holding a framed oil painting towards the light. Jeremy Evans turned the picture around, a warm smile spreading across his tanned face. "What do you think?"

Cows grazing in a field, a thin church spire in the background. The scene looked familiar to Alice. "Was it painted here?"

"Yes," said Eleanor. "That's the church at Little Cornbury." She squinted at the painting. "But those cows are terrible! This doesn't look like the work of a professional artist."

"You'd be surprised what passes for professional work." Alice brushed a finger along the frame. "Though you're probably right that it was painted by an amateur. Did any of your parents or grandparents paint?"

"Wilfred was a keen amateur. Oils, occasional watercolours and drawings. But that doesn't look like one of his."

Jeremy laid the piece on the top of a bowed and flaking chest of drawers. "I found it inside that tallboy, tucked into the bottom drawer. Lordy, people put things in the strangest places."

Eleanor wandered amongst the furniture, opening the doors of a Victorian wardrobe and the drawers of a delicate dressing table. She patted the back of a torn flower-patterned sofa, releasing puffs of dust into the air. "What on earth will we do with all this?"

"Most of these pieces are in good condition," said Jeremy. "That wardrobe for instance. They can be sold at the Narebridge auction. Mr Burridge will arrange to collect them. You'd get a fair penny, I'd say."

"Good idea," said Eleanor. "But what about the rest? The leg on this sofa is broken, and the chest looks a bit rough."

"I can fix up some of the pieces, though I think that sofa's beyond repair."

"Excellent." Eleanor clapped dust from her hands. She took Alice downstairs and into what looked like the living room of somebody's house. A couple of easy chairs huddled around an oil heater and a large kitchen table dominated the back of the space. There were curtains at the windows and carpet on the floor.

"Jeremy doesn't live here, does he?" said Alice.

"No." Eleanor laughed. "But we thought he should have somewhere comfortable to work and rest as he spends so much time here. Nick and I used to follow him around the grounds, but when he came in here for a break, there was nowhere for us to sit. We persuaded our parents to kit it out properly for Jeremy and his visitors. That's to say, me and Nick. And put in some heating too."

"It's a real home from home. There's even a gas ring. Does Jeremy cook too?"

"His wife Sarah packs him a lunch every day. She makes soups and stews which he heats up here. She used to make treats for us too, which Jeremy kept in that old Walker's shortbread tin on the shelf. I suppose he keeps his own snacks there now." Eleanor rapped the side of the tin. "Anyway, Nick and I would sit at the table while Jeremy brought over the tin. We could barely contain ourselves as he took off the lid and we discovered what was inside. Jeremy was like a kindly uncle to us and we loved him dearly."

Alice remembered her own pseudo parent, Aunt Tracey. Alice and Christian had loved their visits to their aunt's home in Sussex. Alice would be excited for days beforehand. She would picture her bedroom there, with its pink wallpaper and the stuffed giraffe she had won in a raffle. Unable to carry it home on the train, it had remained at Aunt Tracey's, a friend always waiting for Alice to return. A steaming dish of home-cooked shepherd's pie would await the siblings, the traditional meal for their first evening's stay.

The days following would be a whirl of trips to the beach, barbeques in the garden and games with their three cousins. Alice joined a riding club, and cantering with the others along the deserted beach, she found she could forget about her absent father and dysfunctional family.

"I've loaded the bigger paintings into the wheelbarrow," Jeremy said from the doorway. "I'll take them down to the house for you. There's more in those boxes on the table. I think they're light enough for you to carry. The rest are in the back room."

Back at the Hall, Alice inspected the paintings. There were variations on the cows in the field picture, some with sheep, and all had the same tarnished, clunky frames. There had better be some higher quality works in the collection or there would be little to hang in the hotel …

Eleanor wanted Alice to start the inventory in the attic. Through a door at the end of the first-floor corridor they climbed a bare, steeply ascending staircase that opened into an attic stretching the length of the house. A vaulted ceiling provided enough height for a giant to stand up straight. Sunshine streamed through one of a pair of large round windows at the two ends. Sturdy oak beams divided the attic into three sections.

"Wow, I was not expecting this."

"It's something, isn't it? Wilfred designed the attic so he could indulge in his hobbies and not bother anyone else. He sketched, painted, studied plants, crop rotation, all sorts. He also took a lot of photos and developed them himself."

"The pursuits of a Victorian gentleman!"

"And that's exactly what he was. He was the only child of a real Victorian and I believe that father and son shared many interests. Wilfred was also an older father. He was in his fifties when my dad was born, so he was very set in rather old-fashioned ways. He kept everything, as you can see. Goodness knows what you'll find here."

"I'm looking forward to sorting through it." She pointed into the first section. "I'm glad to see from those framed watercolours that you have some lovely pieces."

"Wilfred painted those. But over there are the artworks that were on the walls when we lived here. They were all packed and itemised before the builders moved in. I've marked a couple of pieces that I'd like to rehang in the hotel, but otherwise I'll be guided by your recommendations."

Alice wandered over to a leather-topped desk, hugging the wall in the middle section of the attic. The size of a kitchen table, the desk had trays of writing paper, pens and a pile of unrecognisable trinkets.

Eleanor sat on a faded chaise longue, and Wilson jumped onto her lap. "Most of the furniture up here was my grandfather's. After Wilfred's death, my father bought that office chair, intending to use the attic himself. But in the end, he didn't come up much. Too far away from the family, he said."

Alice sat beside Eleanor. "When will the interior decorator be here? I'd like to talk to her about her design."

"Not for a couple of days; she's been held up on a job in Milan. But you can start the inventory anyway." Eleanor rubbed her hands and looked over Alice's shoulder. "Alice, there's something else I wanted to discuss with you." She took a deep breath. "DI Salisbury told me that Nick was shot at close range. To get that close to him, his killer is likely to have been someone he knew. But everyone at the party, Alice, was family or close friend."

"Nathan is an experienced detective, so if that's what he said, I'm sure he's right." The thought of being killed by a relative jabbed at Alice's stomach.

"But I can't believe that one of my guests, someone I know Alice, shot my brother. Why would they? I can't make any sense of it."

Alice held Eleanor's arm. "I'm sure DI Salisbury will find the culprit."

"But how quickly? I want whoever did this caught and I don't want to wait." Eleanor pulled a handkerchief out of her pocket. "I know you solved the Jason Marley case before the police did. Everyone was talking about it. I want you to help me find Nick's killer. Please." The wrinkles around Eleanor's eyes deepened as her eyes narrowed.

How had an art curator managed to get a reputation as a class A sleuth? It was true that Alice had got ahead of the police on the Marley case, but she had not appreciated how widely that fact was known.

"Do you know if Nick had any enemies? Anyone who would wish him harm?"

Eleanor looked at the floor. "Well, there is someone. Simon Newgate, Nick's business partner. Nick's known him for years and he brought him along to some of our family events. But I never trusted Simon. Not after ..." Eleanor dabbed her eyes with her handkerchief. "Well, I just don't trust him. Anyway, he was at the party on Saturday, though he didn't stay long. Actually, I don't remember seeing him again after we found Nick."

"Eleanor, I would like to help you, but I'm sure the police have everything under control. I don't want to hinder their investigation."

"I know what you're saying, Alice, but I'm desperate. I've just lost my only sibling and I want his killer caught quickly. Simon's known us a long time, but *I* don't really know *him*. I always told Nick he should hire another director to keep an eye on Simon."

"What makes you think that Simon would have killed Nick?"

"Jealousy. Simon was in awe of Nick. And Nick's relationship with Devi drove Simon crazy."

Alice could imagine the two men arguing over gorgeous Devi Dutta. Ironically, that was one of the themes of Devi's last movie too. But was it really the motive for Nick's murder?

"I understand this is difficult for you, Eleanor, but we are talking coldblooded murder. You would need to have a very good reason for suspecting Simon."

"And I do." Tears were collecting in Eleanor's eyes again, but she shook her head and sat straighter. "To set up the business, Nick put up sixty percent of the money; Simon was supposed to provide the rest, which he promised Nick he had. All their planning was done on that basis. But at the very last minute, Simon said he couldn't get the full amount. Nick was furious, but he was committed to the venture, so he contributed more. Simon only put in ten percent in the end."

"That is odd." Alice picked up Wilson who had migrated onto her lap and put him on the floor. "Did Simon offer more money at a later stage?"

"No. Simon left Nick with practically all of the risk. I felt that if he could welch on such a big promise right at the start of their partnership, he just couldn't be trusted. And … This is difficult to say out loud, but I always felt that Simon was waiting for an opportunity to get rid of Nick and run the business himself."

Having just started her own business, Alice knew how angry she would be if a partner had let her down so badly. And how that would damage her trust in them. Had it caused ongoing bad blood between the partners? Or had Nick Carberry shrugged it off, only concerned with getting his new venture off the ground? Alice could well understand Eleanor's suspicion, but she had enough on her plate already.

"Eleanor, I'm sure that if you tell DI Salisbury about Simon Newgate, he will do a thorough investigation."

"I know he will. But there'll be the full glare of a police investigation and stories in the local media. I can't take that kind of publicity at the moment and nor can the hotel. You could talk to Simon quietly and he wouldn't know that you suspected him. He'll be more open with you than with the police." Eleanor clutched the edge of the chaise longue. "I have to know who killed Nick. And with your reputation, you're the only person I can trust to get a quick and discreet result."

Chapter 5

ALICE WAS FLATTERED THAT Eleanor had asked for her help, but she was not getting involved. Her previous dalliance with a murder investigation had taken a toll on her day job. Joe had been constantly worried for her safety, unhappy when she had insisted on pursuing the case. But Joe was not her boss. And it had been an undeniable thrill when she had solved the murder before the police. If she managed her time better, perhaps she could fit in a small investigation after all. What was the harm?

Eleanor seemed very sure that Simon Newgate had killed her brother, so Alice would start there. She dropped Christian back at *Daisy*, where she did some research on Nick Carberry's company.

Nick had set up Carberry & Newgate Advertising six years ago, with Simon Newgate as creative director and junior partner. They opened a small office in London's Golders Green which went well. Then they moved to Narebridge, where lower rents meant a bigger office and more staff to service their growing business.

The agency looked to be thriving. It had a stable of well-known companies on its books and a web page of testimonials from business leaders. But it was Nick's face that sold the agency. There were pictures of him with clients, accepting industry awards and attending celebrity parties. Nick had got the lion's share of publicity and attention.

Simon Newgate came across as a quiet backroom presence. Perhaps that had fuelled his jealousy. Alice decided to pay Simon Newgate a visit at the Narebridge office.

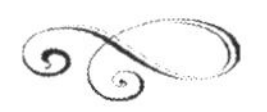

Alice was led into a spacious conference room, decked with posters from the agency's campaigns. She sat at the board table and had already drunk half a cup of very good coffee when Simon Newgate burst through the door.

"I'm sorry to keep you waiting." He pulled out a chair beside Alice. "I've got a new client who needed a bit of hand holding."

Alice recognised the tall man with bushy red hair from the Carberrys' party. He had been in the library when Alice arrived, talking to Eleanor's cousin Harry.

"I really just popped by to say how sorry I am about Nick," said Alice. "It must be hard for you being back in the office so soon."

Was that too leading? Eleanor had said she wanted a discreet investigation.

"I stayed at home yesterday, but it was agony." Simon rolled his lips together. "Better to keep busy."

If it had occurred to him that her visit was slightly odd, he showed no signs of it.

Alice turned away from Simon's pained expression. "This is such an impressive office, how long have you been here?"

Simon looked around the room, brown eyes wide, as if seeing it for the first time.

"Five years. We needed a bigger office and we picked Narebridge as both Nick and I were brought up in the area. And Great Wheaton is only ten miles away, so it's a shorter commute for me." Simon folded his arms.

"But you also have a London office."

"That's to keep our presence in the capital. It's a tiny office, just a gateway to here where all the action takes place. But Nick was based there, as he was the agency's best salesman."

"I thought he was chief executive."

"Well yeah, that too. But his main remit was to find new business opportunities. Then it's down to me to come up with creative campaigns."

"And that was an amicable arrangement? Nick staying in London and you being here?"

"Absolutely." Simon looked at Alice directly for the first time. "Nick loved London. The pace, the buzz, being in the centre of everything. And of course, he lived there. But I prefer the laid-back vibe out here. There's a cool creative scene too."

It seemed to Alice as though Simon was selling her her own home town. "So, what will happen to the London office now?"

"Tristan, one of our account managers, will man Golders Green for the time being. In due course we'll do an assessment as to the office's value to the business and make a decision on what to do going forward."

"It seems you already have a plan worked out."

"We're never without a plan."

"But a plan for when your partner dies? That seems a bit morbid."

Simon frowned. "Put like that, I suppose it does. But we're a business and we need contingency plans to cover every eventuality. Including the death of one of the partners."

"I see." Alice was not sure that she did see. She finished her coffee and replaced the cup in its saucer. "I met Devi Dutta at the Carberrys' party. It was thrilling to meet a real-life Bollywood star. I suppose you must know her well."

Simon's frown deepened. "Of course I do. It was me who introduced her to Nick. She was looking for an ad agency to launch her new clothing brand in the UK. She contacted us and as Nick was away, I took the call. I met her for a preliminary chat and by the time Nick got back, I had Devi signed up."

Alice remembered Devi saying that she was here because of interests other than filming. Alice thought that meant seeing friends or visiting the local sights. She hadn't imagined that Devi had her own clothing line.

"She's a canny businesswoman." Simon smiled. "Anyway, Nick made a beeline for her the minute he saw her. The next thing I knew, he'd whisked her off for a weekend in Paris. And when they came back, she moved into his flat."

Alice wriggled her toes in her Vans. "I see." And this time, Alice did see.

Alice heard music as she jumped off the gangway onto *Daisy's* deck. Strings and winds, an infectious beat, forced Alice's hips to sway as she pranced down the companionway. Christian was doing the same thing in the saloon. When he saw Alice, he grabbed the remote and turned down the volume.

"I'm watching *The Sunny Girl*. Devi is so good and what a brilliant dancer."

Alice pulled off her Vans and chucked them onto a pile of shoes by the companionway. "Where did you and Devi disappear to, Christian, while I was with Eleanor?"

"She gave me a tour of the house and told me about the refurbishment plans. She wasn't exactly full of the joys, as you can imagine, but I think she was grateful for the distraction. It's such a fantastic house, perfect for a boutique hotel. Devi has lots of ideas for decorating the place. She has great taste." Christian's arms flew around him.

"Devi seems to have had quite an impact on you."

"She's a remarkable woman. An accomplished actress and an astute businesswoman. Do you know she designs her own clothing range?"

"I just found out."

"I was telling her about my plans to travel. I've always wanted to go to India and I'm planning a trip there. She was so encouraging. Told me I could stay with her and she'd show me around."

Alice laughed. "You are kidding me, big bro. You don't seriously think that you and Devi …"

Christian huffed and ran a hand over his glossy hair. "Anything's possible."

Alice stood up and retrieved her shoes. "Look, there's no food here, so why don't you come and have lunch with me at The Coffee Pot?"

"Thanks, but I think I'll get an Indian takeaway and watch the end of Devi's film." Christian brushed by Alice and ran up the companionway.

Alice was still staring after him with an outstretched hand, when Roddy Rafferty appeared in the open doorway.

"Dear girl, bless you! It's been years since I had that effect on a woman." Roddy grinned. "And that's before I've shown you my surprise. Come on up."

Alice stepped onto the deck to find her round metal table laid with a whole fish, a dish of salad and a stick of French bread. Beside it, a bottle of wine cooled in a bucket of icy water.

"I thought I'd treat you to lunch for a change." Roddy pulled out a chair and placed a faded linen napkin on Alice's lap. "I caught the fish this morning up at Little Cornbury."

"What a lovely surprise, thank you, Roddy. What fish is this?"

"A brown fish." Roddy served Alice a portion.

"It tastes amazing."

"Barbequed it as soon as I got it home, the best way to cook fish." Roddy filled their glasses. "So how is life chez Buchanan? Going well I hope."

"Yeah, it's good."

Roddy stroked his cheek. "Though the tone of your voice suggests otherwise."

"No really. It's fine."

"Forgive me for persisting, but your jutting chin confirms that there is something bothering you."

Rats! How did the man know? Alice put down her fork and leant back.

"Nothing's wrong. It's just that I've lived on my own for a while and I'm struggling to adapt to living with someone else."

"A sharing problem. Is it the space or the bathroom products?"

"Joe is as light as me on the products. And it's not the space either; I have *Daisy* if I need some space. It's more … the fact of it."

"Living with someone, anyone, can be difficult. But you just need to persevere. It will get easier."

"I'm sure you're right. And Joe is so laid back."

"So commitment phobia slain?"

"I hope so. But it's early days and I don't want to jinx our relationship."

"Joe is unjinxable. And if he's not, I'll get my voodoo doll out and stick pins in it." Roddy broke off a piece of bread. "I see Christian's settling in okay."

"He may have settled in better than I anticipated. He came with me to Renton Hall this morning, took one look at Devi Dutta and he was gone."

"Well she is a Bollywood star. You can hardly blame him, she's quite something."

"She is. But her boyfriend's just been shot and she'll be going back home to Mumbai soon."

"Things will run their course on that front. However, this murder business: What do you make of it?"

"I'm glad you asked." Alice told him about her conversation with Eleanor Carberry and her visit to Simon Newgate. "The killer had to be one of the guests at the party. Eleanor's convinced it was Nick's business partner, but now that I've met him, I'm not so sure. I mean, he was a bit shifty, but he works in advertising!"

"With Nick gone, Newgate might end up owning the whole company, wouldn't he? And if he's someone who doesn't like being told what to do, that has the makings of a motive for murder."

"But Nick Carberry brought in lots of business and the company was doing great. Why kill the golden goose?"

"That is the other side of the coin. Fascinating ..."

"Isn't it? But I don't even know where to start." She saw Roddy arch an eyebrow beneath his straw hat. "Okay, I do know where to start. Get as much information on the victim as possible. I know next to nothing about Nick. What do you know about the Carberrys, Roddy?"

"Not a great deal, other than that they are a wealthy family who live in a big house. But I have a reliable pipeline to the local gossip if you would like me to tap into it."

"Yes please, that might be helpful. But don't let it interfere with your own work. You've got your exhibition soon."

"Dear girl, if I've learnt one thing in life, it's to let everything interfere with your work. It will get done of its own accord."

"If only my freelance business would run itself."

"It will eventually, but it needs a bit of nurturing at the beginning." Roddy walked across the deck and leant against the barge's side. "If you're not going to finish that bread, your swan friends are over here looking for lunch."

Four fluffy cygnets fought over the crumbs Alice threw in the river, watched over by their elegant mother.

"I was thinking," said Roddy. "Bumping off your business partner at a family party is the perfect cover. All those people coming and going, a darkening evening, a wood. It has all the ingredients for a perfect murder mystery."

"That's true." Alice wiped crumbs from her hands. "Actually, I've just remembered. There was a blond man who called Nick away while I was talking to him."

"Really? Who was he?"

"No idea. He whispered something in Nick's ear, then Nick excused himself and left. That was the last time I saw him alive."

Roddy twirled a strand of grey beard. "Very interesting. So we need to track down a blond-haired man and find out what he said to Carberry."

Alice looked at her friend. "Do you know, Roddy, I think you're enjoying helping me solve these murders."

"Do you know, Alice, I think I am."

Chapter 6

A MORNING MIST CREPT over the fields and kissed the surface of the water as Alice walked beside the river to *Daisy Dawn*. She had got up with the birds, woken by Joe gathering his equipment together for a two-day photography assignment in Edinburgh.

Taking advantage of the early start, she had answered emails, especially those asking for quotes on new projects. Chasing after work was a new experience for Alice. She had spent all her career in the comfort zone of regular contracted employment at art galleries. Now that her reputation in the field was growing, she hoped that the Renton Hall project would lead to more opportunities as a freelancer.

A murdered client on her shift, however, was not going to enhance her resumé.

Alice stopped at the market, where she sated her sweet tooth at Marilyn's Candy Stall. She picked up a bag of the week's special, chocolate and lime candies, testing a few before she reached *Daisy*.

Christian emerged from the cabin, dressed in a tailored linen suit, crisp white shirt and red and yellow striped silk tie. Alice looked down at her shorts and navy t-shirt. She had still to master the art of freelance dressing.

"You look ridiculously smart. Where are you going?"

"With you of course, to Renton Hall." Christian's voice lifted. "As it's such a big job, I thought you needed a full-time assistant. And I've already met Eleanor."

Alice moved empty Curry House takeaway boxes from the counter, reaching underneath for a black rubbish bag.

"I don't need an assistant, Christian. And aren't you supposed to be sorting out your own life?"

"I can do that while I give you a hand. Besides, it gives us the chance to spend more time together."

The truth was that Alice knew she would enjoy it too. "In that case, you can help me get organised. I need a couple of A4 pads, some sellotape and lots of different coloured felt tips; they're in that pencil case on the coffee table. Also, I'm going to photograph the collection for the inventory and I've brought one of Joe's cameras. Would you mind checking that the battery's charged? If not there are some spares in one of the drawers in the sideboard."

Christian flitted between the saloon and the cabin, gathering things up, while Alice unplugged her laptop and slotted it into a case. Roddy's head appeared at the hatch door.

"Is it safe to come in?"

"Absolutely," said Alice. "Come on down and tell us how your painting's going."

Roddy helped himself to a flying saucer from the sweet jar on the coffee table and settled on the sofa.

"Slowly. Painfully. Expensively. But mostly slowly."

"Oh. Sorry to hear that. But you've done solo exhibitions before, so you know what's involved."

"Dear girl, it's been years since my last one-man show. And I don't remember there being this much work. The show is supposed to open in a few weeks and at this rate, I'll hardly have anything to display."

Alice perched on the sofa's arm. "Is there anything I can do to help?"

"You can be your usual engaging self, Alice. The rest I'm going to have to do myself." Roddy's brown eyes twinkled.

"How many paintings do you need?"

"I can't bring myself to say the number out loud. But enough to fill both downstairs rooms at Gregory's House."

"Gosh, I see the size of the problem. What's the theme again?"

"Regional landscapes, luckily, which gives me plenty of scope. There'll be other local artists upstairs too." Roddy slipped off his flip-flops. "I've got the painting I did of the river out here recently. And I'm doing some sketches of the fields opposite, but I'm stumped after that."

"Why don't you come with us to Renton Hall?" shouted Christian from the cabin. "There's loads of pretty scenery around the grounds."

"I wasn't planning to put any dead bodies in my pictures. But now you mention it, it would create a talking point!"

"Roddy, that's terrible," said Alice. "Even by your standards."

Roddy threw up both hands. "I stand admonished."

"He's right, though, it's lovely at Renton Hall. Why don't you come with us and have a scout around for ideas?" Alice lowered her voice. "Christian's hijacked my assistant's spot, but really it's so he can see Devi again. He's got the hots for her."

Roddy shifted closer to Alice. "Tell me about it. I came over here last night to ask Christian to turn down that appalling music – I'm sorry Alice, but Indian music just doesn't shake my tree. And I ended up staying half the night, while he wittered on about Devi's movies and something about clothes."

"You could have just left him and gone home."

"I know, I know, but at first I didn't want to abandon him. He appeared so bruised and vulnerable after being dumped by Jasmine. Yes, I got that story too. And then I discovered he'd found an instant cure …"

Their laughter brought Christian out of the cabin. He searched their faces for signs of the joke.

"Okay Christian. It's time to carry my bag."

Built in the eighteenth century, Renton Hall had already experienced fire, neglect and lavish attention by the time that Wilfred Carberry bought the house in 1913. Over the years, the Carberrys had modernised the interior, introducing television, double-glazing and microwave ovens. But when Alice drove the Defender between two stone lions at the end of the driveway, she entered a landscape that had barely changed in two hundred years.

Lush grass edged both sides of the drive, turning into fields filled with glowing, gilded wheat on her left hand side. On the right a wood, the outer edge marking the border with the neighbouring property, ran up to the house a hundred yards ahead and wrapped around the back.

A pheasant shot out of the trees and across the road, gold speckles on its back shimmering in the sunshine. Alice braked when a second bird followed and she watched it amble across the driveway to join its mate. Outside the house, men in white overalls emerged from two vans. They took out ladders, buckets and tins of paint, setting them down at the front door of the house.

Roddy sauntered around the side of the house while Alice and Christian picked their way over plastic sheets in the hallway. They were about to make their way to the attic when Eleanor called out. "Alice, can I have a quick word before you start, please?"

Alice put her laptop on the stairs. "Christian, would you mind going over to Jeremy's snug and checking that all the paintings he found have been brought down to the house? I have a feeling we may have left a box behind."

Christian slung the camera bag over his shoulder and made for the conservatory, running a soft hand over his quiff.

"Gina Salvini, our interior decorator, is coming today and she wants to talk you through her design plans." Eleanor twirled her hand around a knob at the foot of the bannister. "We've agreed that her team will start here in the reception area."

"Good, I'm looking forward to meeting Gina."

"And one more thing. I'm having lunch with Harry and Cheryl and I'd like you to join us. I'm hoping they'll take a more active role in the project now. I don't think I can manage the whole thing by myself." Eleanor looked into the distance. "Without Nick."

In the attic, Alice folded her arms, leant back against an oak post and looked through the round gable window. Outside, a pair of ducks nestled into the grass on the edge of the stilled lake. It was still inside the stuffed attic too. Alice looked around, wondering where to start.

She made for the pieces that had previously hung in the house. Georgian landscapes in oil with spidery cracks; vibrant pots of flowers; spare contemporary abstracts; family portraits. The usual eclectic choices that formed most of the private collections Alice had seen.

She opened a spreadsheet and typed in information about each piece. Title, artist, date and any other facts she thought Eleanor would want recorded. Alice unwrapped each work, took a photo on her phone, typed up the data and re-wrapped the picture. Whilst fascinating, it was repetitive work and with nobody to talk to, Alice found the local radio station on her laptop. She turned up the volume and sang along.

Paintings logged, Alice moved on to a row of boxes on a shelf. She opened the first one, filled with items wrapped in newspaper. She had just released a copper sculpture of a tramp from its covering, when Eleanor appeared in the doorway.

"I called you from the bottom of the stairs and it wasn't until I was half way up and heard the music, that I realised why you couldn't hear me."

Alice rushed to the laptop and paused the radio. "I'm so sorry, it was louder than I thought."

"It must be a bit lonely up here on your own – I would have done the same thing." Eleanor picked up the tramp sculpture. "I thought this was the ugliest thing I'd ever seen when my father brought it home. It sat on a little table beside mother's armchair in the drawing room. I used to hide it behind a big lamp. Ghastly little thing."

"I'm not mad on it either I must admit, though there's a market for these. It will probably fetch a couple of hundred pounds at auction."

"Good. I'll give it to Jeremy and he can take care of it, along with the furniture." Eleanor put the sculpture back in the box. "I came to tell you that Gina Salvini has arrived and she'd like to meet you."

They found Gina in a corner of the library, a mobile phone held to one ear. A petite woman with a tight dark bun and dark-rimmed glasses, her free arm flew around her as she talked. She spotted Eleanor and signed off with a brusque, "Ciao."

"Tsk," said Gina. "Suppliers, they are the same everywhere. They promise you they can move the earth and then they tell you that moving the earth is impossible." She grasped Alice's outstretched hand. "I am delighted to meet you, Alice. Eleanor has told me about your job here. We will work well together I think." In her heavy Italian accent the word came out as 'tink'.

"I'm looking forward to seeing your plans for the hotel."

"There is no need for writing. It is all in here." Gina tapped her head. "I will tell you my plans."

"I've already put aside a couple of good paintings," said Alice. "I thought they could go in here."

"They will not be required. I have briefed my dealer in Paris, who will source the perfect artworks for you."

Gina's message that her own art recommendations would not be required, caught Alice unawares.

"But I thought we could use some pieces from our own collection," said Eleanor, her cheeks reddening. "We have some fine artworks."

"We don't want fine." Gina threw both arms in the air. "We want magnificent, we want extraordinary. We want a hotel with artworks fit for a king."

A hotel for kings in Great Wheaton! Alice lowered her head to hide a smirk. But when she looked at Gina again, she could tell the designer wasn't joking.

Eleanor stepped within arm-waving distance of Gina. "But, I wanted—"

"I promise you will get a hotel beyond your wildest dreams. Just leave everything to Gina Salvini."

Chapter 7

ALICE SAT AT WILFRED Carberry's desk in the attic, staring at her computer screen and still smarting from Gina Salvini's brush-off. Of course Gina was in charge of the decorating – she was the designer, after all. But Eleanor had specifically told Alice that she should propose artworks from the family's collection. It was Eleanor and Nick's wish for the new project to have a strong link with the original family home.

And that was the part of the job that Alice had been most looking forward to. It was a big project in her new freelance career and Alice wanted to learn and experience as much as possible. She had hoped that she could persuade Eleanor to accept enough recommendations to cover the whole hotel. She needed case histories for her website and the Renton Hall project would be the perfect endorsement. She wanted to appeal to people who needed help arranging their own paintings, as Alice thought that much of her business would lie in that area.

Was Gina a control freak? Or did she just want to hike up her fee?

Alice turned to the paintings that Jeremy had found in the hayloft, now jumbled together in an old chest. Alice picked through them, sneezing as she released a cloud of dust. She held out an oil painting of a wonky yellow bowl. It contained apples a shade of green that apples should never be and a bunch of chipped marbles masquerading as grapes.

The artworks were all old, and some were torn or with damaged frames. Several were just too terrible to consider hanging. But not the Margaret Thomas. A dreamy oil painting of wild flowers in a simple white jug.

"What is a little pearl like you doing in the reject box?"

Alice turned over the image and on the back of the canvas, read the message written in green felt tip.

To Eleanor, Congratulations on your wedding. I wish you and Tom many happy years together. Love Simon N x

Underneath the message was a little sketch of a bride and groom.

Simon N. That must be Simon Newgate surely? Alice ran light fingers around the frame. It was smooth – there was no sign that fittings had ever been attached. The painting had never been hung. Perhaps it was not to Eleanor's taste. Alice re-examined the image. At the very least it was inoffensive. Surely Eleanor could have found a spot to hang such a pleasing gift?

Or perhaps it was the giver that Eleanor did not like. It seemed that Eleanor's distrust of Simon went back a long way. When Alice had met Simon, she had sensed an unattractive touch of envy over Nick Carberry's relationship with Devi. But what man wouldn't be jealous? Devi was a stunning Bollywood star. It surely wasn't enough to drive Simon to murder?

Beeps from the radio announced the midday news. Alice gathered up her bag and went downstairs. Eleanor was in the reception area, watching two men as they rolled Magnolia onto the walls.

"Gina thought this area should be clean and plain. I agree, as we've got a couple of lovely watercolours of the lake that I'd like to hang here." Eleanor fiddled with a button on her shirt. "If Gina doesn't mind, of course."

Gina strode out of what would soon be the hotel's dining room, but was for now the stripped-down family drawing room. She finished her call and pointed with her mobile. "Carpets, Eleanor. Something elegant but stainproof where people are eating. Is that so hard to understand?" Gina threw hands in the air and glared.

Eleanor smiled in sympathy. "We're just heading off to lunch now; you'll join us won't you, Gina?"

"I never eat lunch." Gina put her hands on narrow hips, showing her black-and-white houndstooth Chanel suit to its best advantage.

Eleanor fiddled the button right off her oversized plaid shirt and put it in the pocket of her sludge-coloured cargo trousers.

"But I *will* stop for an espresso. I've brought my own machine," said Gina. "That is enough. We must work hard if we are to meet the opening date in a few weeks, no?"

The Bull Hotel was one of the oldest buildings in Great Wheaton. A coaching inn during the fifteenth century, it still served fresh, locally produced food for regulars and visitors. The restaurant, housed in what was once the stable block, was packed as usual. But there was no missing Cheryl Horton.

"Over here, Eleanor," she shouted, waving both arms.

Alice recognised the woman who had so dramatically announced Nick Carberry's death at the party, as she followed Eleanor to the table by the window. Cheryl rearranged the chairs so they could all see the high street as it humped over the River Nare.

"Sit yourselves down and I'll get you a drink." Cheryl took Eleanor's bag and hung it over the back of her chair.

Cheryl bent forward as she sat down, her low-cut leopard print top struggling to contain her bulging bosom. A thick layer of foundation covered her bony face, her watery blue eyes were rimmed with kohl. There were pink streaks in her blonde hair. "We're all here. Good. I'm starving."

Harry passed Alice a menu. Heavy pouches under his eyes protruded from his pale face. He put a hand over his paunch, while his other hand held on to the stem of a wine glass as if he would never let it go.

"First of all, Eleanor," said Cheryl. "Me and Harry are delighted you've asked us to be involved with the refurbishment. I've always said Renton Hall would make a lovely hotel, haven't I, Harry? And I've got a few ideas for the décor."

She opened up a piece of paper and gave it to Eleanor. "This is a design for the main bedroom. It's the biggest room with the best view, so it needs special attention. You won't have to worry about standards," – Cheryl patted Eleanor's hand – "I only want the best and I warn you, I'll push everyone hard. But as Cher would say, 'I'm only difficult if you're an idiot.'" Cheryl laughed loud enough to bring disapproving glances from a couple on the next table.

Eleanor smiled at the couple. "Thank you, Cheryl, but we already have an interior decorator. And Nick and I have agreed the design and colour scheme."

"We're here to support you, Eleanor," said Harry. "We want to see the project completed the way you and Nick planned. It will be Nick's legacy."

"Thank you, Harry, that's a lovely way of seeing it."

A waiter brought drinks and took their food order.

"Talking about Nick," said Harry. "How's the police investigation going? DI Salisbury came to see us yesterday, asking questions about our statements. Any idea what that's about?"

Eleanor opened her mouth to answer, but Alice jumped in first.

"DI Salisbury is very thorough. I expect he wanted to clarify something. At this early stage, he's just gathering information."

"But it was the second time he'd questioned me."

Alice scanned Harry's face. Nathan must have had a good reason to question Harry a second time.

"As I say, I'm sure he just wanted to check something."

Bowls of chilled melon soup were presented. Alice picked up her spoon and tucked in.

Harry said: "I'd have thought the police would be concentrating on Simon Newgate. He's got to be the prime suspect, hasn't he? He's always been jealous of Nick and he runs that agency as if he already owned all of it."

"It was Nick's idea to stay in London and let Simon look after the main agency out here," said Eleanor. "It suited them both."

"I'm surprised you're sticking up for Newgate," said Harry. "Especially after the Jamaican invoices episode."

Alice's spoon stopped in mid-air. Was this the reason for Eleanor's poor opinion of Simon?

"That all got sorted Harry, didn't it?" Cheryl shot Alice a hard stare. "Just a misunderstanding. That sort of thing happens in all companies."

Alice sensed Eleanor stiffen. The Hortons' attention turned to their soup. It seemed a good time to take a comfort break.

The cloakrooms were on the other side of the hotel, so Alice trod across creaking boards and into the bar. A blackened, double-fronted stone fireplace was the room's most attractive feature, though a basket of pine cones did not have the same effect as wintry orange flames. A couple of older men with rowing club ties and double whiskies, sat on deep leather armchairs on either side of the hearth.

Alice was admiring a new addition to the bar's collection of etchings when she heard a familiar laugh. She peered around the fireplace and saw Christian and Devi tucked into the far corner. Heads close together and talking in whispers, they did not notice her. What was Christian doing, flirting with Devi in such a public place, so soon after her boyfriend's unexplained demise? Alice stepped forward, hand outstretched ready to tap Christian's shoulder. On second thoughts, Christian's love life was none of her business. She retraced her steps and used the first-floor bathroom instead.

When she returned to the table, the others were tucking into lasagna. A portion at her place was already cooling.

"I forgot to say congratulations, Harry," said Eleanor. "Cheryl told me that you were made partner."

"They should have done it years ago." Cheryl stroked Harry's cheek. "I kept telling Harry to push himself forward more. Promotions don't happen by themselves."

Harry blushed, his red cheeks turning a shade redder. "Thought they'd get to me eventually," he said.

"But you're forty-three! Two of the partners are in their twenties."

"Still," said Eleanor, "not everyone gets that far, so well done, Harry. I suppose more responsibility will keep you in the office longer. Do you really think you'll have time to help with the hotel?"

"Absolutely. Renton Hall is a priority for me, Eleanor. Of course, I won't be able to be on site all the time. But I'm at the end of a phone and I expect you to call me whenever you want to."

"Don't you worry." Cheryl laid an arm across Eleanor's shoulder. "You can count on the Hortons. We're always here for you."

Eleanor reached into her bag for a tissue and dabbed her eyes. "You're all being so kind. I didn't know how I was going to cope without Nick; I thought I'd have to abandon the project. So thank you for your support." She turned to Alice. "You too, Alice. What you're doing for the family is really important to me."

"It's my pleasure." Alice glanced at her watch. "I wonder how far Gina's team have got while we've been away?"

"We should go back and check on them," said Eleanor. "Gina is determined to meet the opening date, but she is so ... determined."

"I should hope so," said Cheryl. "That's what she's being paid for."

"First things first." Harry threw his napkin on the table. "Nick's killer has got to be caught. I want to see that deplorable Simon Newgate behind bars."

Chapter 8

A LONE ROWER POWERED through the water as Eleanor drove along the river road. Harry and Cheryl chatted in the back seat. A cool breeze blew across Alice's face. She closed her eyes and turned towards the open window.

Cheryl had insisted on paying the bill for lunch. She had also urged Alice to visit her at her office in London. They should be friends, Cheryl had declared with such authority, that Alice accepted their friendship as a foregone conclusion. But it was Harry's repeated assertions that Simon Newgate was Nick's killer that occupied Alice's mind. Harry was *so* sure of it. Neither Harry nor Eleanor appeared to have even entertained the idea that there could be another suspect. And those Jamaican invoices? There were no Jamaican clients on the Carberry & Newgate Advertising website.

As Eleanor pulled up outside Renton Hall, two tradesmen were carrying a roll of carpet out through the entrance. Eleanor got out of the car and, still holding onto the door, shouted across the gravelled car park. "Where did that come from? All the carpets earmarked to be replaced have already been taken away."

One of the men dropped his end of the roll inside a van and walked over. "Miss Salvini told us to get rid of it. She said there'll be a new carpet for the library."

"There most certainly will not." Eleanor slammed the car door and marched into the house.

Alice gathered her bag and by the time she got inside, Eleanor had collared the designer.

"Gina, I thought I'd made it clear to you that the library carpet was staying. We only had it fitted last year. And it still looks new."

Gina wound a finger around a long chain necklace. "Tsk. New or not, it does not fit the ambience I am trying to create. That green, so dark and depressing, it was like walking through a forest in a storm. The window here is small, so we have to create light with our design. A pale carpet, Eleanor, will fool the eye into thinking it is a joyous spring morning."

Alice snorted louder than she intended. Whether she was too far away for the women to hear or they were too engrossed in their conversation to notice, neither gave her the disaproving stare she expected.

"I hear what you say." Eleanor clasped her hands in front of her chest. "But we haven't budgeted for another carpet."

"Quite so. But we fiddle, no? The total price will be the same in the end."

Eleanor dropped her hands by her side. "Oh! Good. Well in that case, carry on. But next time, please consult me first before you make any changes to the plan."

Gina turned towards Alice and clapped her hands. "Alice, now is a good time for us to talk. Come into the library please?"

Drooping clouds and a small window contributed to the library's gloom, though the bare, pale floorboards made the room seem bigger. Whilst Gina may have made a dramatic move, she was right about the carpet.

"So, we'll create here a welcoming space for guests to read or relax beside the fire with logs. None of those old men's leather chairs. So uncomfortable. And those titchy round tables with skinny legs? Tsk, you couldn't rock a cat on one of those. That's how you say, no?"

Alice smiled. "I know what you mean."

"We need a special painting to go above the fireplace. Something colourful I think, but not too bright. Not too big, but not too small. There must be action, but not an abstract. Interesting but not too detailed. My dealer with find something."

Good luck with that, Mister Dealer!

Gina led Alice through the rest of the house, arms thrusting left and right. Colour schemes, furniture, accessories and more new carpets. Fragrant soaps for the bathrooms, padded hangers for the wardrobes, superfast broadband; no detail was too small for Gina.

Alice ran her hand around the porcelain sink in the main bedroom's en-suite bathroom. She turned on the tap. Eleanor had mentioned that there had been problems with the water pressure, but a clear flow of liquid gushed out at Alice's touch.

"And Alice, when will you finish the filing?"

Alice gripped her fingers around the tap. She glared at Gina's back, as the designer fiddled with a sash window's lock. "Filing?"

"The family paintings. You are filing them, no?"

Alice shoulders relaxed. "Oh, you mean cataloguing? Yes, I'm doing an inventory of the artworks in the house.

It'll probably take a couple of weeks to produce the final report." Alice craned her neck past Gina and peered out of the window. "Eleanor asked me to look at a crate of ceramics she found in Jeremy's snug, so I'm going to head up there before it starts tipping down."

Gina spun around, eyes wide. "The gardener's house is falling down?"

Alice laughed. "No, I mean it's going to rain."

Gina turned back to the window. "Tsk, this English!"

Alice jogged over the bridge and along the side of the paddock. She dived into Jeremy's snug just as the clouds broke and rain pelted down. Shaking drops off her arms, Alice flicked the light switch by the door and picked her way to the room at the back of the building.

Used by Jeremy as a storeroom, shelves were stacked with weed killer, coils of wire and trays of bulbs. In an organiser along one wall, tiny drawers held nails, screws, bolts and hinges, different sizes and a range of colours, marked with neat red labels. Alice found two boxes on a handmade work table in the centre of the room.

Both Eleanor's parents, she gathered, had been keen on ceramics. Mary Carberry had taken some of her favourite pieces with her to Scotland, but the rest of the collection was now wrapped in newspaper awaiting its fate. Eleanor did not share her parents' passion for ceramics, but she wanted Alice to see the pieces. Though whether Alice would get any of her recommendations passed the fiery Italian was another matter.

Alice unwrapped a delicate art deco-style vase with a red mephisto design. It was interesting in a kitsch way, but it would not go with the sophisticated design Gina was going for. Next was a smudgy grey skull, with yellowing teeth and a peacock blue bandana around its forehead. Alice shivered and unwrapped another piece.

She held up a thin clay bowl. From a stumpy base the size of a bottle top, misty sage-coloured sides morphed into dove grey, billowing wide and ending in a perfect circle. Grey splodges speckled the outside and the inside was a dusky cream. This one was definitely worth a fight with Gina.

Alice inspected the remaining items and found a couple of other pieces she liked. She re-wrapped them and placed them in one of the boxes. They would go back to the house with her, but first she wanted to have a nose around the hayloft. There was some fine furniture up there and Alice now had time to examine them properly before Jeremy took them to auction.

Alice climbed the outside steps. The stone treads were slippery from the recent downpour and she clung onto the steel railing. Black clouds clung to tall treetops and occasional raindrops slid off leaves, dropping to the floor of the wood. A pair of squirrels chased each other along the path, where only a few days earlier Nick Carberry had lain dead.

Crack! Alice jumped. Just a branch creaking. But she had bashed her shin on the edge of the step. The door was slightly ajar. Alice hesitated. She looked over her shoulder but there was nobody around. Placing her palm in the middle of the door, Alice eased it open.

It took a moment for her eyes to adjust to the gloom. She walked one hand along the inside wall, but failed to find a switch. Pulling the door fully open brought more light to the front of the loft; enough for Alice to make out the wardrobe she had seen before. One step further inside, she grabbed a sideboard for support and eased across the floor.

Mould spores filled Alice's nostrils and she sneezed. Reaching into her pocket for a handkerchief, she caught herself in a dressing table mirror. Alice fingered the ornate metal border around the oval glass. She crouched down, as if sitting on a stool, and tipped the mirror so she could see her face and shoulders. As she fiddled, what looked like the tread of a boot appeared at the bottom of the glass.

Alice spun around. She dropped onto one knee and grabbed a leg of the dressing table. She squinted at the tread. The boot. Steadying herself, she rose and took her mobile from her pocket. Switching on the torch, Alice took a half-step and ran the beam over the boot. It was attached to a leg. Which was attached to a body. Which was very still. Indeed.

Alice held the phone at her shoulder and the light shone wide enough to make out the features.

Jeremy Evans.

Chapter 9

As far as Joe Buchanan was concerned, Alice was the untidiest person on the planet. He repeatedly said as much. Alice tried hard to be tidy, but she had not yet found a reason to doubt Joe's assessment. Until she walked into *Daisy*'s saloon.

Shirts hung over the curtain rail. CDs, separated from their cases, covered the sofa. Takeaway cartons spilled over the bin to the floor, the drainer was stacked with dirty crockery. Alice did not remember Christian being so untidy when they were children.

She opened a cupboard in the kitchen to get a broom. As she went to close the door, her hand brushed against a corkboard tucked between the wall and a vacuum cleaner. Alice had used the board for her previous investigation. Thinking she should be tidy for once, she had pinned her notes onto what she called her incident board. And it had helped her to see all the information graphically presented in one place. It worked then, it could work again.

Alice cleared the sideboard and propped up the board, brushing off the cobwebs that clung to the cork. She reached for her laptop case and took out two photos. She pinned Nick Carberry's head and shoulders at the top of the board and a picture of Simon Newgate beneath it. An image of Jeremy Evans flashed through her mind. Alice had no doubt that the gardener had been murdered too. And just feet from where Nick had died. Alice did not have a picture of Jeremy to hand, so she drew a quick sketch, wrote Jeremy's name underneath it and pinned it alongside Nick on the board.

Two victims.

The hatch door clicked open and Christian lumbered down the companionway, bulging plastic bags in both hands.

"Don't bother clearing up the mess, Ally, I'm just about to sort it."

Alice put her hands on her hips. "Just so you know, I wasn't going to clear it up."

Christian appeared not to notice. He dropped bulging bags on the floor and took off his jacket.

"I've invited Devi over for dinner this evening. I'm doing an English. She told me that people always take her to Indian restaurants when she's here, so she never gets to eat popular local dishes."

"And you're cooking ..."

"Spaghetti Bolognese." Christian took some dirty mugs from the sink, turned on the taps and rolled up his sleeves.

"And that would be the English version of the Italian spaghetti Bolognese, I assume?" Alice picked up a tea-towel.

"I said popular local food. And we're all Italian now."

"But Devi's Hindu isn't she, so she can't eat beef?"

"She's vegetarian so I'm using Quorn. I make a good veggie sauce, if I say so myself. And I'm doing trifle for dessert which *is* English."

"I thought you didn't like cooking."

"I used to hate it. When I first moved in with Jasmine, she cooked so I didn't have to. But when she started working late in the evenings and I got bored with sandwiches, I learned to cook for myself. I was surprised to find that I really enjoyed it."

Alice looked at the empty cartons from Livvie's café on the floor.

"It seems you decided to take a cooking break here?"

"With Livvie's great food and the café so close, why would you ever cook yourself?"

"That's my excuse, too."

Brother and sister matched CDs to cases and cleared debris from the furniture. Alice sat down while Christian unpacked his shopping. He opened a bottle of red wine and poured two glasses.

"Salut." He handed a glass to Alice.

"Cheers."

Roddy rapped on the hatch door and crossed the saloon to collect the glass Christian offered him. On the way, he saw Alice's corkboard.

"Dear girl, do I detect the makings of another incident room?"

"Incident room?" Christian tapped Nick Carberry's picture. "Into Nick's death? I'm intrigued. But why are you doing the investigation and not the police?"

"A very good question," said Roddy. "And the answer is, that your sister is so good at it."

"Ably assisted by one Mr Roddy Rafferty I might add."

"And you should add," said Roddy.

Alice wriggled to the front of the sofa and put her glass on the coffee table.

"Not just Nick," she said, "but Jeremy too. That pathetic drawing of mine – is supposed to be Jeremy. They were both murdered at Renton Hall and if the killer isn't found soon, Eleanor can forget about bookings for the hotel."

"I wouldn't worry about that," said Roddy. "There are plenty of people who would find that kind of notoriety appealing."

"Plus, I'm working there all day and I don't want to be the next victim."

Christian put a hand to his mouth. "You don't actually think someone is after *you*?" He turned to the board. "Though they will be, once they find out you're doing this. And what about Devi? Do you really think this investigation thing is a good idea?"

"The sooner the culprit is found, the safer we'll all be."

Alice noticed her brother's troubled expression and decided to drop the murder conversation. She moved away from the board and sat down on the beanbag beside the coffee table. Roddy squatted beside her and opened the sketchbook he had brought with him.

"If I may change the subject for a moment," said Roddy, "I would like your opinions on some ideas for my exhibition. They're not worked up properly – some are just a few lines – but there's enough to give you an idea of what the finished work will look like." He opened the sketchbook and pushed it across to Alice. "Be honest. On second thoughts, be kind."

Christian knelt beside Alice and they examined the pencil drawings. The little humpback bridge lacked detail but was instantly recognisable. As was the river scene near The Shepherdess pub. Less familiar was a stretch of river with an empty bench in the foreground and the base of a big oak tree to the side. It occurred to Alice how poignant a few pencil lines could be.

"Where is this, Roddy?"

"In my imagination! That one's more of a concept piece."

"I love it. It's very moving. Will you paint it in oil?"

"I don't really have time to finish many oils so this will be a watercolour."

Alice looked up at Roddy. "Interesting. I don't think I've seen any of your watercolours before."

"That's because I've barely done any. I hope I'm not being too ambitious. If I can't master the techniques, half the show will be terrible."

"I'm sure you won't have too many problems. Besides, these sketches are lovely, you could always use some of them."

Roddy beamed. "What a good idea. A couple of sketches would bring variety. I was worried that a monotheme might be dull."

There was a buzz from Christian's mobile. "Oh my God, I should at least have made my trifle by now!" Christian turned off his alarm and shot up.

"I'll help you," said Alice. "What time is Devi due?"

"Soon."

"Ah, a romantic dinner for two," said Roddy. "In which case, allow me to assist."

Devi insisted that Alice and Roddy stay for dinner. What would be the point of them being alone in separate empty homes, when they could all spend the evening together? And there was plenty of food. Christian scowled at Alice behind Devi's back. But despite Alice's half-hearted attempt to leave, Devi would not be moved. She was not going to turf anyone out, especially family.

Alice enjoyed the meal – Christian had done well to whip something up so quickly. Her own cooking skills were legendarily bad, indeed non-existent according to Joe. For some reason, he didn't count heating up prepared meals as cooking ... Alice had promised that she would improve. Joe had even offered to teach her and he was an excellent cook. But all that peeling and chopping. And that was on top of reading and understanding the recipe. For goodness sake, how was Alice to know that sautéed potatoes had nothing to do with salted ones?

Devi loved the food, especially the trifle which reminded her of a dessert her mother used to make. Christian took Devi's praise with an enormous smile and gushing thanks. Though he grew increasingly impatient with the lavish attention Roddy got from his special guest.

Devi was fascinated by Roddy's sketches. As fellow artists, albeit in different disciplines, the pair had a lively discussion on techniques and the value of practice. Many hours in Devi's case and almost none in Roddy's. They talked about their latest projects and Devi outlined the story and songs of *The Sunny Girl* sequel that she would begin shooting next year.

Roddy had never seen a Bollywood musical. Christian found a clip of one of Devi's dance numbers on YouTube and they watched it on Alice's laptop.

"That's marvellous," said Roddy. "So energetic. But so complicated. I don't know how you remember all those moves, Devi."

Devi tossed her hair over her shoulder. "Actually, it's not that hard. The backing dancers do sequences like that all the time. We learnt that routine in two days."

"You are joking, of course."

"No, many of the steps repeat. And as this is a fast number you don't notice that I made a couple of mistakes."

"But you're so graceful," said Alice. "I wish I could move like that."

"Here, I'll teach you." Devi jumped up and stood in the centre of the saloon. "Come and stand next to me."

Neither Alice nor Roddy needed asking twice.

"Both arms to the left and step to the right. Shake both shoulders." Devi demonstrated. "Jump to your left and thrust out your hips. One, two."

Alice jumped to her right and banged into the coffee table.

"Let's move the furniture and we'll all do it together."

They moved the sofa and coffee table against the wall and Devi pushed the beanbag into the corner. She organised Alice, Roddy and a reluctant Christian into a line and they did the movements again.

"Not bad for a first attempt. Let's give it another go." Devi stepped in front of the others. "This time I'll be out front, so you can follow me."

If only. Alice jumped, swayed and shook. Just not in the right order. Roddy swore that he was born to "Bollywood dance". Christian and Alice agreed they were both hopeless, preferring their dance moves confined to darkened places.

Devi was picking up a cushion from the floor when she spotted Alice's incident board. "I see you've started your investigation into Nick and Jeremy's murders."

Alice held up her hands. "It's not what you think."

"You don't have to pretend, Alice. Eleanor told me she'd asked you to investigate Nick's murder." Devi put a finger on her chin. "I see you have Simon Newgate down as the suspect."

"Well ..." Alice felt herself blush. "I'm keeping an open mind, but it does seem that Simon has a motive. He wanted to get Nick out of the way so that he could run the business himself."

A frown clouded Devi's beautiful face. "Perhaps, but if it were me, I'd have Harry Horton's picture up there."

"But he's Nick's cousin. And from what I've heard, they got on really well."

Devi sat on the arm of the sofa. "They did get on well. But Harry was jealous of Nick and jealousy pushes people to do extreme things."

Alice could not imagine Harry Horton doing anything extreme. Devi must have noticed Alice's puzzled expression.

"I can see you're not sure, so meet me tomorrow and I'll tell you more about Harry."

Christian poured himself another glass of wine and leant against the counter. "I admire your enthusiasm ladies," he said. "But you should leave all this to the police. They will catch the killer without your help."

Alice glanced from Roddy to Devi to Christian.

"Nick and Jeremy were both murdered at Renton Hall while we were there. I've got to find out who did it, or the next victim could be one of us."

Chapter 10

It was only after Alice threatened to throw him out that Christian agreed to vacate Alice's bed and sleep on the sofa. It was well after midnight before Devi and Roddy left and Alice was too tired for one of Christian's strops. Christian had spent the end of the evening sulking. He had watched his dinner date laugh with Roddy and Alice as they swapped stories of difficult artists they had worked with. They had finished off their meal with coffee and followed that with something of a singalong session over the washing-up.

At first, Alice had been sympathetic. She and Roddy *had* ruined Christian's planned intimate dinner with Devi. But did Christian really think that he was at the beginning of a magical relationship with this famous Bollywood star? This was not *Notting Hill*!

Christian probably thought Alice was being harsh, but she was only thinking of her brother. He would be upset when Devi went back to Mumbai and her own life as a movie star, without him. And besides, Devi appeared unruffled by her boyfriend's recent demise; something Alice thought did not bode well on the relationship front.

Alice loved her brother, but sometimes she felt that she hardly knew him. In some ways that was literally true, as they had spent the majority of their adult lives miles apart. They messaged each other sporadically and had occasional chats on the phone, but they only saw each other a couple of times a year. Alice enjoyed the time they did have together, always feeling a pang when they parted.

But she did not know Christian's habits any more. The opinions that annoyed him, the words that wound him up. And last night she had found out that brutal honesty upset him very much indeed.

Alice had slept badly. She pulled back the curtains and watched the first hazy morning rays peek above the horizon. When the cabin grew lighter, she got up and took a long shower. She dressed in navy trousers and a pale blue striped t-shirt.

Alice put her ear against the saloon door. There was no movement from the other side. It was not yet eight o'clock, so she tidied the cabin and Christian's paraphernalia in the bathroom, until there was nothing else left to straighten. She opened the door.

Christian was standing by the counter, fully dressed and looking out the window. Bedding was piled on the sofa just as Alice had left it the night before.

"Good morning, did you sleep okay?"

Christian turned sharply. "No, I didn't. How could I sleep after what you said to me?"

Alice knelt on the sofa, both elbows on the arm. "I'm sorry if I upset you—"

"Upset me!? Upset doesn't even begin to describe how I feel. You dare to tell me that I'm not good enough for Devi. How could you be so cruel?"

"Calm down, Christian."

"Calm down? Is it too much to expect my own sister to be supportive?" Christian held onto the windowsill, as if to prevent his anger from pushing him out.

"All I was saying, was that you shouldn't get your hopes up. And anyway, I hardly know Devi."

"Exactly. So how do you know if our relationship can last or not?"

"How can you? You don't know her any better than I do. I was only trying to point out the reality of your situation. But look, I don't mean to interfere and I'm sorry for upsetting you."

"Hmm." Christian released the windowsill, gave Alice a pointed glare and walked across the saloon and into the cabin. He slammed the door behind him.

Alice made herself coffee and opened her inbox with trepidation. Whilst she was enjoying freedom from company rules and regulations, freelancing came with its own set of anxieties. Most importantly, where the next pay cheque was coming from.

Alice was surprised at how much of her time she was spending chasing new business. She was always sending out proposals and quotes to prospective clients, most of whom did not even bother to acknowledge them. Should she pencil in dates for work that might not materialise? If she did, she would not be available when somebody actually accepted her quote.

The Renton Hall job would take her to the hotel opening in September, but the rest of Alice's diary was filled with pencil marks. She needed to convert some of those potential clients into real ones.

Alice leant back on the beanbag, diary in hand. Two of

the jobs looked more promising than the others. A couple who had just moved into a house on the outskirts of Great Wheaton wanted help to hang their art collection. They wouldn't be ready for a month or so, however. A new pizza restaurant in the town centre was opening in a couple of weeks and the owner had asked Alice to hang some photos. She had not received a response to her quote, so it was time to pay him a visit.

Cows grazed at the water's edge on the opposite side of the river, as Mr and Mrs Swan glided past. Alice waved at Livvie through The Coffee Pot's window and continued along Sam's Lane. At the end she veered off through an alleyway and onto the high street.

Outside the new pizza restaurant, a man was standing at the top of a stepladder pulling on a rope, an oblong box attached to the other end. *Emilio's Pizza*, in solid red letters, blasted out of the sign. His colleagues below inched the box this way and that at his instructions, faces straining with the effort. Alice went inside, where the owner, a short man with a bald head and a piercing voice, directed another team. This one was measuring up for shelves.

"What do you think of the place so far, Alice?" said Emilio Gambi.

Alice took in the varnished black floorboards, the stone-coloured booths and freshly painted walls. However there were cables hanging from the ceiling and the kitchen was visible through a gap in the wall.

"It's looking good. I like your colour scheme, it's clean and fresh."

"Obviously there's some finishing off to do and that's where I hope you can help us."

"You want to hang some family photographs on the walls, I understand?"

"That's right. Here, I'll show you."

They sat in one of the booths and Emilio untied a red ribbon around a large folder on the table. Inside was a stack of black and white photographs, which he passed to Alice.

"These were hanging on the wall of my grandfather's restaurant in Vieste, my home town. Nonno had a big brick oven which took up the whole of the back wall. He made it himself and it produced the best pizzas in the world." Emilio twisted around, clutching the back of his seat, resting his other arm across the top. "I've copied the design for my own oven."

Emilio patted the photos. "Anyway, I've picked out these ones and I want them hung on the walls here. Carry on the family tradition. I've added some recent pictures of my children, too. Mustn't forget them."

Emilio jumped up from his seat. "Let me get you a cup of coffee. I've brought my own espresso machine from home, until I get the big one delivered. While I make it, you have a look through."

Alice picked up the photo at the top of the pile; a young man with an eager face and slicked dark hair stared back. He must be Nonno. In the background, a small balcony looked over a bay lined with fishing boats. There were other family members underneath Nonno's photo, obvious from their striking resemblances. A young boy, a warm smile revealing two missing teeth, leaned into Nonno's enveloping arm.

"That's my dad." Emilio put an espresso cup on the table. "He was seven years old when that picture was taken and he was already working in the kitchen. Just doing a few odd jobs, but that's where he learned the trade. Ten years later, he was running the place."

Emilio moved the prints around with his finger, picking up one with another young boy.

"Me with my son in the same spot. See, there's the bay in the background. My cousin runs the restaurant now; good business he does too. I want to expand the family firm over here."

"There's some lovely pictures here, they'll look good on the walls."

"I'm glad you like them. You'll hang them all won't you?"

Alice sipped the excellent espresso. "These two have faded along one side, they must have been hanging in a sunny spot. They look damaged, but there's not much we can do about it. This one especially."

"Yes, I wondered if you'd say that. No problem, I'll keep Uncle Alfredo at home."

"And this one." Alice held up another photo of Nonno, this time shaking hands with a man in a dark suit sporting a bushy moustache. "It's buckled and torn around the edges, also the corner's been ripped off. And it's faded. I'm not sure we can use it."

"No, no I definitely want this one. That was the mayor of Vieste and Nonno's first customer. Nonno said the photo brought him luck and it always hung in the same spot in the middle of his restaurant. It's going up just here." Emilio slapped the wall above their booth.

Alice examined the photo again. "In that case, I'll take it to the framer and we'll see what he can do with it."

There were clothes hanging from every possible point in Devi's bedroom in The Bull Hotel. T-shirts and pyjamas, neatly folded and arranged by colour, were heaped on the furniture. Devi cleared two easy chairs by the window and invited Alice to help herself to tea.

"I'm so sorry about the mess. I've just received the samples for my new clothing range and I wanted to see them straightaway."

Alice glanced at the blue and white striped t-shirts and straight black trousers flung across the bed.

"They're the sort of clothes I would wear myself. I was expecting your range to be more … colourful."

Devi laughed. "Everyone says that. People expect to see bright Indian colours, saffron and orange especially. I'm always asked about those colours. But these are casual clothes that work better in more muted colours. And they sell better, too."

Alice reached for a t-shirt and rubbed the material.

"It's soft, isn't it?" said Devi. "All my clothes are made from good quality material. I don't expect to pay good money for a sub-standard product. The cotton is grown in India."

"Are the clothes made in India too?"

"Some are made in Kolkata and some in a factory in Bangladesh. But others are produced in Europe. I want to create jobs in different regions."

"And the launch? That'll be in London, I assume?"

"The first one, yes. And that's coming up soon. There'll be other launches in New York and Mumbai afterwards."

"What made you decide to branch out of acting and into clothing?"

"It's not that much of a stretch really." Devi crossed lithe dancer's legs. "When I began my acting career, I made my own costumes because I had to. When I worked on bigger movie projects, I helped to design my outfits. One day, I was playing with drawings of clothes that I wanted to wear off set and decided to make them up. Devi Dutta Clothing was born."

She poured a cup of Assam tea. "You must come to my launch, it's going to be at a restaurant in Soho. I'll show you a picture." Devi rifled through a stack of photos on the windowsill and handed one to Alice. A tuxedo-clad Christian leered out at her.

"It was your brother's idea. See, there are steps up to a balcony that runs across the back of the restaurant and down the other side. Christian thought I could use it like a catwalk. The guests would be able to see the clothes properly and it's a great backdrop for pictures."

It did look an ideal location.

"I like your brother." Devi wound strands of wavy hair around her finger. "He's full of great ideas. I keep telling him, he should come to Mumbai with me and set up a business. It's the entertainment capital of India with lots of creative people, he would fit in really well."

Alice's eyes ran over the Bollywood star. Beautiful, talented, successful and sweet-natured. It was hardly surprising her brother had fallen for Devi. And Christian deserved a loving relationship. Even so …

Alice should mind her own business and let whatever was going to develop between Christian and Devi, run its course. But Alice's self-contained mother was not a big part of her life and her father had abandoned the family long ago. The thought of her only sibling skipping off miles away to Mumbai made Alice feel nauseous.

"I promised I would tell you about Harry Horton." Devi got up and slammed the window closed. "The high street traffic is so loud! That's why Renton Hall is such an ideal spot for a hotel."

"You're right, it is peaceful there." Alice picked up the teacup. "Apart from the odd murder, that is."

"And why was Nick killed? I'm sure you want to ask me. Well, the answer is because Harry was jealous of Nick."

More jealousy? Was there anybody around Nick Carberry that was not envious of him?

"Nick was always talking about Harry, he was very fond of his younger cousin. Although it was always clear that Nick was the leader – and Harry seemed happy enough to tag along. Actually, Harry has spent most of his life following Nick around." Devi moved a gold bangle around her wrist. "The Hortons and Carberrys are close families. Harry is an only child and both his parents worked, so Harry would spend his school holidays at Renton Hall. Nick said that Harry tried to stay as long as he could."

"Ah. Now I see why he's so attached to the place. He practically grew up there."

"And he was close to Nick's mother too. Nick told me that his mother was not the most ... maternal of women. But she felt sorry for Harry. She made sure he had good food and plenty to do when he stayed at the Hall."

The Assam was good, and Alice poured herself another cup.

"Once they were adults, the two men's lives diverged. Nick went into advertising and, as you know, set up his own successful business. Harry went into law and has been at the same firm for the past twenty years, his entire career in fact. Nick had a wide circle of friends, some of whom are celebrities, whilst Harry lives a quiet village life."

"I don't see how a different life translates into a motive for murder."

"I agree, it's not obvious. That's because Harry had become so good at hiding his feelings towards Nick. But the fact is that Harry was consumed with jealousy. He wanted to be Nick, to have everything that Nick had. I've seen Harry a lot over the past few months and I saw all the signs. Harry copied the way Nick spoke, the way he sat. He pretended to be interested in the things that Nick enjoyed. And I know for certain that Harry was jealous of my relationship with Nick – he told me so one time."

There was a knock on the door. "Food at last." Devi carried over a plate of fruit. "Please help yourself."

Alice selected a slice of mango and dipped it into a pot of yoghurt. "I'm sorry to ask you, Devi, but about your relationship with Nick …"

Devi kicked off embroidered silk slippers and tucked her legs onto the chair. "I was looking for an advertising agency to launch my first clothing line and I invited C&N to pitch some ideas. I loved their approach and I have to say, I liked Nick straightaway." She blushed and pulled her hair over her cheek. "Anyway, the launch was a big success. The agency had worked hard and I was delighted with the results. Nick wanted to take our relationship further, and I was pleased that he felt that way because I liked him. Though I didn't think I could be his girlfriend and his client at the same time."

"I understand. That's a tricky combination."

"Nick felt the same way. But as the launch project was finished by then, we were no longer working together. But it did mean that he couldn't pitch for any future business from me."

"Which is why your latest launch is being handled by another agency." Alice licked yoghurt from her fingers.

"Yes. Our relationship continued, but just between you and me, Alice," – Devi leant forward and patted Alice's knee – "as much as I liked Nick, it was difficult having a long-distance relationship. We wouldn't see each other for weeks and when we did meet up, we were together all the time. It was exhausting. In fact, I told Nick that I couldn't carry on, the week before the party."

"But you still went. And, if I may say, you looked like you were still a couple."

"Nick asked me to go. He didn't want to let Eleanor down. Anyway, at the family dinner the evening before, Harry made some inappropriate comments about me and Nick. And then he said a terrible thing." Devi looked out of the window for a moment. "We were talking about Nick's plans to open a new office in Dublin, when Harry said: 'Your ambition will be the death of you.' Everybody else ignored him, but he said it with such force, it scared me. Especially when he repeated it just as I was leaving. I felt that I needed to stay close to Nick."

Devi's dark eyes turned liquid. And for the briefest of moments, Alice wondered whether the tears sprung from the woman or the actress.

"What about Jeremy Evans? Did Harry kill him too?"

Devi's forehead creased. "You mean the gardener? I don't know what Harry would have had against him."

But she didn't rule out Harry as Jeremy's killer. Interesting!

"But as for Nick ..." Devi grasped Alice's arm and looked straight into her eyes. "Alice, I'm absolutely certain that Harry meant to harm Nick. Harry Horton is the murderer."

Chapter 11

A BLUE TIT FLITTED along the hedgerow, keeping pace with Alice's pony as it plodded along a narrow path beside a corn field. After promising to book herself a ride, Alice had finally arranged a hack at Farrell's. She was riding Patches, the pony she saw regularly in a field near *Daisy.*

Despite the lapse of time since her last ride, Alice had quickly found the rhythm of the pony's stride. She relaxed into the saddle, enjoying the patchwork of fields that stretched out to the horizon. Patches followed the instructor's horse around a stack of newly harvested wheat, through a gap in the hedgerow and into the adjoining field. They cantered to the other side, the wind rushing against Alice's face. Patches stretched his neck and pushed on faster, hooves thundering on the ground. Alice felt her heart gallop too and she almost whooped out loud. She pulled up and eased out the reins, and they joined a path beneath the trees and headed for home.

Alice patted the pony's black-and-white-patched neck. She thought of the photo she had seen of Devi standing beside a similar pony, while modelling her clothing range. The shot was one of several in a brochure produced by

Nick Carberry. The glossy pages had perfectly showcased the range and had become a hit on social media, proving Nick's accurate reading of the market.

The actress's assertion that Harry had been jealous of his cousin all his life, and was waiting for the opportunity to kill him, seemed far-fetched indeed. Why would Harry have waited for the night of the party, anyway? He must have had plenty of less public opportunities to bump off his cousin.

Could it be a classic case of the good-looking, successful man and the not so bright, can't get the girls, embittered cousin? Hardly – Harry had been successful too. He was married, apparently happily, and had just been promoted. Harry's slow rise to partner did not seem to have impressed Cheryl, but forty-three seemed a reasonable age for promotion to a senior position in a law partnership.

And then there was Simon Newgate. Presumably he would get the whole business now, as everyone seemed to assume. Although Simon, too, could have found a less dramatic way of getting rid of his partner.

Alice did not want murder to spoil her ride. She ran her hand along Patches' neck and ambled back to the stables.

Back at Joe's apartment, Alice showered and dressed. In the spare room, she opened the wardrobe and took out her Mary Potter painting. She gazed over the little brown jug remembering how she had bought the artwork from an online auction. The next day she had fretted over the cost; far more than she could afford. But when the painting had arrived, it was even more beautiful in real life and she had never regretted her purchase. The painting had become her favourite.

Alice had brought the work with her intending to hang it up in Joe's apartment. She had hesitated. Hammering a nail into Joe's wall was so … permanent. But she should make more of an effort to adjust, so she took the painting through to the living room.

Joe's desk was in the corner of the room, the shelves above held folders of photographs and books on the craft. He had originally intended using the spare bedroom as an office, but he preferred the light from the balcony's glass doors and the view over the river. The room was sparsely, but tastefully furnished. Framed photographs lined the walls. Alice had always liked this room and the Mary Potter work would fit in perfectly.

She attached the fitting to the wall and hooked up the painting. She was straightening the artwork when a key in the lock broke the silence sooner than expected. A bag thudded on the floor.

"I didn't expect to see you here." Joe took off his leather jacket and hung it on the back of a dining chair. "Afternoon off?"

"I took a break and went riding. Now I'm winding up to start work again."

"I see you've hung up your painting. It looks good there."

"You do like it don't you?"

"I do. And that's a good spot for it." Joe put his hands on the back of the sofa and stretched.

"Sore?"

"Crouching all day to shoot chickens has played havoc with my back."

"Chickens? I thought you were at a wedding."

"I was. In a barn. They wanted a country touch. So I took pictures of chickens, the bride, the bridesmaids, then more chickens."

"They'll look at the photos in five years and wonder what they were thinking of."

"I don't doubt it. Still, it pays the mortgage. Did I miss anything while I was away?"

"Jeremy Evans was murdered. At Renton Hall."

"Jeez!" Joe walked across the room, opened the balcony door and looked out.

"But as to why … Eleanor and Nick adored him and I don't think he could have had an enemy in the world."

Joe turned around, hands on hips. "Well, he had at least one. And if you carry on snooping around, you may find yourself going the same way."

"I won't if I get to them first."

"I don't know why you even take the chance. That Salisbury guy has things in hand and I'm sure he doesn't appreciate you getting involved. Besides, won't it cut into your work? The Renton Hall job is big enough."

"I've thought of that and I can juggle things. I'll complete the job on time. Look, you don't have to worry about me. Honestly it'll be fine."

Joe gave a wry smile. "So who's the poor devil next in line for one of your interrogations?"

"I should have a chat with the person who knew Jeremy best. His wife."

Joe crouched beside Alice. "If you really must hunt down killers in your spare time, please be careful."

Sarah Evans' pink-washed cottage lay at the bottom of a tree-lined lane on the edge of Little Cornbury, the village between Great Wheaton and Renton Hall. Butterflies danced over pink roses in Sarah's vibrant garden. Beneath a pergola dripping with purple foxgloves, Alice tucked into Sarah's homemade apricot cake.

"The milk was fresh from the farm next door." Sarah poured tea from an elephant-shaped teapot. She folded papery, gnarled hands around a sodden handkerchief.

"This is lovely cake. Eleanor told me about the snacks you used to make for her and Nick when they were children."

"I'd always pop something in for them when I was packing Jeremy's lunch. I don't think they had much in the way of treats in the big house."

"Oh, I got the impression that their parents were generous."

"The Carberrys were nice people, don't get me wrong, but Mrs Carberry was a bit of a puritan. Scottish you know." Sarah raised an eyebrow over tired, grey eyes. "She didn't allow eating between meals and she made those poor children wait until six o'clock for their tea. I mean, they were starving by then, so I just gave them something to keep them going."

Alice smiled, remembering that when she was a child, her mother would not allow sweets in the house. Christian would sneak chocolate bars into his sports bag and offer to wash his football kit himself. Their mother was only too happy for one less job to do and Alice and her brother would stand beside the washing machine, gorging themselves.

"The apricots in the cake, are they from the tree in the front garden?"

"Oh yes, we had a lovely crop this year, I'll be making apricot slices for weeks." Sarah glanced in her lap. "Though who'll eat them all I don't know."

Alice touched Sarah's knee. "Do you have any family nearby?"

"I have two daughters who live in Coldbrook, so they're only ten minutes away. I look after the grandchildren during the holidays." Sarah's face brightened a little. "I used to take them up to Renton Hall to play in the woods."

"I know that Jeremy looked after the grounds there, but what did that mean exactly? I don't know anything about gardening."

"Well it was Mr Carberry, Eleanor's father, who brought Jeremy to the Hall. Jeremy was working in a garden centre, the Bolder's Farm place around the corner on the main road. Mr Carberry went in there one day wanting advice on remodelling his garden. Jeremy went to the Hall to see what needed to be done and Mr Carberry offered him a job overseeing the work. That was forty-one years ago now."

Alice felt pressure on her calf, as a black cat rubbed his neck on her trousers. "Was that when they got rid of the cattle?"

"It was. Jeremy worked on the gardens around the house, especially the vegetable plot. They planned to expand it, grow different varieties. Mrs Carberry wanted the family to be self-sufficient. They even brought in chickens. But they kept wandering off and laying eggs all over the place, so Mr Carberry got rid of them."

"So, Jeremy would have been there when the decking around the lake was installed?"

"That was Jeremy's design." Sarah cocked her head to one side, the sunlight catching the bags beneath her eyes. "The old Mr Carberry, Eleanor's grandfather, had the conservatory put on the back of the house. But you walked straight onto the grass, which only brought clippings into the house. Jeremy said the decking would be neater and cleaner."

"He was right. That lake area is fabulous. I guess Jeremy designed the little bridge over the stream too?"

"Save you wobbling on those planks, he said. Jeremy had a real talent for landscape design."

The cat jumped onto the bench beside Sarah and peered at Alice over the cakes.

"Sarah, please say if it's too much, but I wanted to ask you about Nick Carberry. I don't suppose Jeremy knew who might have wanted to harm him?"

Sarah pursed her lips. "If he did know, he didn't say anything to me. But Jeremy wasn't there that night, so it's not as if he saw anything."

"He didn't mention whether Nick had any enemies? Anybody who held a grudge against him?"

"Nick had his own company and as I see it, when you make a success of your business, you're always going to make somebody unhappy."

Alice pictured Harry Horton. His envy must have made him unhappy. Now that she thought about it, she could not remember ever seeing Harry really happy. He smiled and socialised, went through the motions. But the smiles didn't reach his eyes and his shoulders looked as if they carried a kitbag of troubles. Harry would go to the top of the suspects list.

"Such a lovely boy Nick was. Always chirpy and so grateful for everything you did for him. He used to send me little notes to thank me for the snacks. I've kept them all. I'll show you."

Sarah fetched a shoebox from the house and picked out a crumpled sheet of pale blue paper. Using different coloured pencils, a young Nick had thanked Sarah for the 'smashing' jam tarts. He had drawn a picture of a red-centred pastry in the corner of the page.

"It's adorable! What a sweet thing to do. And you kept so many of them."

"I've kept them all. Eleanor's too."

On impulse, Alice asked: "What do you think of Harry Horton, Sarah?"

Sarah rolled her eyes. "Dearie me, what a sulk that boy was. Trotted after Nick the whole time and always looked like he was carrying the weight of the world on his shoulders." Sarah leant forward as if afraid of being overheard. "Mind you, being an only child and dumped at the Hall all through the holidays must have been upsetting. I expect at times he would rather have been in his own room at home."

Sarah rummaged through the box picking out random notes and passing them to Alice. With her free hand, she dabbed at her eyes with the handkerchief.

"I'm so sorry, Sarah. One more question. Do you think it possible that Harry could have killed Nick?"

Sarah clutched the box. "It's possible I suppose. But I don't think the man has the gumption."

"How about Simon Newgate, Nick's business partner? Is he a likely suspect?"

"Perhaps, though I don't know him that well."

"I think it must have been one of those two, though I'm not sure about their motives."

Sarah put the shoebox on the table. She took both Alice's hands in her own.

"Heavens, child, there's only one motive. Nick Carberry was killed because of the dog."

Chapter 12

Alice turned the Defender onto Narebridge Road, inching along behind a tractor until it veered off into a field. She picked up speed, two jars of Sarah Evans' chutney knocking together on the front seat as she drove over a hole in the tarmac.

Sarah had finished their meeting with a tour of her allotment. She told Alice about her interest in propagating vegetables and herbs. Squashes were her speciality. Orange ones, yellow, curly and striped specimens. But Alice was not thinking about vegetables. She conjured up an image of Wilson, Eleanor's Yorkshire terrier. Was this dog the motive for Nick Carberry's death?

The little animal had been Eleanor's pet for the past two years, after she brought it home from an animal rescue centre. Now that her teenage children spent more time away from home, Eleanor had begun to feel lonely. The dog had become a big part of her life, accompanying her from home to Renton Hall, belted into his own seat in the back of her car. Wilson had the run of the Hall and its grounds, although he was rarely more than a few feet away from his mistress or, more recently, the new garden sculpture Nick had shown off at Saturday's party. For a reason that nobody could fathom, Wilson had found a spot he liked at the front of the statue's plinth, snuggling himself beside the marble instead of his usual place by Eleanor's feet, when she sat on the decking.

Someone killed Nick Carberry because of this little animal? It must be some special dog! But Alice had not wished to press Sarah Evans on the matter, so she drove down Renton Hall's driveway none the wiser.

Two coats of paint had lightened the reception area. One of the decorators, on his knees glossing the skirting board, shouted a cheery greeting. Alice could hear Gina Salvini's voice coming from the dining room, so she peered around the door. Gina was speaking bullet-speed Italian into her mobile, as she watched two men unhooking a glass chandelier from the ceiling. An ornate affair, with curly candle holders and strings of crystal balls like pearl necklaces, the chandelier was an eccentric feature of the room.

"So old-fashioned," said Gina.

It was not until Alice turned to leave that she realised Gina was talking to her. "The light fitting. So old-fashioned."

"I suppose it is. It must have been here for years. Are you replacing it?"

"Certainly. Still with glass, as Eleanor wants, but something less fussy. A striking piece all the same."

Gina beckoned Alice and showed her two green squares painted on the wall. "I can't decide which colour for this room. As it looks over the lake and the wood, I think a pale green. This one is called willow tree. And this one, apple white, is lighter. Which do you prefer?"

There was little to distinguish between the two squares, but Alice plumped for the fractionally paler shade.

"Hmm." Gina swung the gold chain around her neck. "The darker one, I think."

Alice retreated to the attic. A plan chest in the back corner was calling to her. Wilfred Carberry had stuffed the drawers with bits and pieces, according to Eleanor, but as nobody had been near it for years, she had no idea what was inside.

At first, Alice had been excited at the prospect of rummaging through the old and neglected chest. She imagined finding a rare piece that would stun the Carberrys and the art world. But then reality bit. She thought it more likely she would find unfinished sketches and unpaid bills, along with bits of orange peel and mice droppings.

She decided, instead, to try a tall mahogany display cupboard with half-glazed doors. She turned the key in the lock and opened both doors wide. Rows of glass shelves from top to bottom housed a collection of antique hand guns, pill boxes and silver spoons.

Guns with milky bone handles and delicate silver filigree. Petite oval and round boxes; silver, wood, some with painted lids. And the spoons. Each with a different scene painted on square ends.

Alice traced a finger around a pill box, enamelled flowers covering its sides. As she went to pick it up, she accidently knocked the shelf above. Before Alice could do anything to stop it, the shelf crashed down. Precious items tumbled to the floor, settling amongst shards of glass.

Alice ran down to the kitchen to find something to clear up the mess. She spent the best part of an hour picking up splinters of glass and polishing off antiques. Fortunately, none of the items were damaged, but Alice had to rearrange the whole cabinet in order to fit all the items onto one less shelf.

The waist-high plan chest, wide and deep, suddenly looked more attractive. Alice pulled out the first drawer and laid it on the top of the unit. Just-begun sketches, watercolours on curling paper, notepads full of numbers, balls of string, tins of pencils. It was, indeed, stuffed with stuff.

Alice turned on the radio, opened up a new spreadsheet and logged the contents. Tucked at the back of the drawer she found some sketchbooks, Wilfred Carberry's name written on the front. Alice opened one of them, and the distinctive heart-shaped white face and small beak of a barn owl glowered at her.

There were pheasants in another book. Proud red and blue faces, topped with brilliant copper plumage and speckled tails. Grey females led lines of chicks across the page. In another were insects: spotty ladybirds, leggy grasshoppers, snappy beetles. The drawings would make an amazing exhibition on their own. If they were framed properly they would look good in the new dining room. But could she get them past Gina? Could she get anything past Gina?

Wilson raced across the floor and jumped on the chaise longue. Eleanor was close behind him. "We came to see how you were getting on." Eleanor stroked the sketchbook in Alice's hand. "I see you've found some of Wilfred's drawings. He was mad about animals, so you'll find lots of books like that."

"They're beautiful drawings. He was a talented artist."

"Wilfred was talented in many areas and that made him a hard act to follow. Though my father tried to please him, he always felt that he was a disappointment to Wilfred. The only talent Dad had was making money."

Alice closed the sketchbook and put it with the others on the desk. "If you could only choose one talent, that's a good one to have."

"I suppose so. And because of it, I got to live in this lovely house."

Eleanor rummaged through the drawer. She took out a piece of brittle paper, a watercolour painting of a heron wading through a lake. "This was painted at my Auntie Ann's property in the Scottish Borders, she's my mother's sister. That's the lake at the front of the house. Wilfred used to wander over the estate, filling those books with sketches of hares, stags, birds, anything he encountered. Then later, he'd work them up into paintings."

"Do you have any of his paintings here?"

"Not the Scottish ones. He gave them to Auntie Ann and she hung them in her house. There's a fabulous oil painting of a kestrel in flight, at the top of her staircase."

Alice took the paper from Eleanor and uncurled the corner. "It sounds the perfect place for an artist. Do you visit there much?"

"Mum used to take us every Easter and again in September. The grounds are wonderful. Nick and I would cycle off in the morning with a packed lunch and stay out until it got dark. We'd build hideaways in the woods and swim in the lake. Though ..." – Eleanor whispered behind her hand – "we weren't supposed to." Eleanor smiled. "Let's see what else is in those drawers." She scooped out an armful of papers. "Just old invoices by the look of it. I'll sort them out at home."

Wilson paced along the wall sniffing at the skirting board, his tail fanning the air.

"Goodness me, here are the plans for the estate." Eleanor lifted out a large sheet and carried it over to the desk. "That black line is Renton Hall's boundary and here's the house right in the corner. The land goes over to the west and north."

"How much land is there altogether?"

"One hundred and ten acres. It was originally only eighty, but Dad added more. The Jacksons, our neighbours on the north side, divided their land up before they sold it and offered Dad first dibs. We should frame this and put it in the porch."

Alice put a hand on Eleanor's shoulder. "Will you tell Gina, or shall I?"

Daisy's saloon was tidied and hoovered. There were no clothes slung over chairs in the cabin. There was no evidence of Christian at all. He had gone without saying goodbye. Alice felt as if Patches had kicked her in the stomach. Alice sat on the bed, hands over her face, and dropped onto the duvet. She should never have stuck her nose into his relationship with Devi. And now he was so mad at her, he had left.

Alice's relationship with Christian was complicated. As children, they had rarely fought, but they had not been particularly close either. As the older sibling, Christian grew tired of Alice trotting around after him. He was more outgoing than his sister and with his growing army of friends, he was out a lot. Spending ever more time on her own, Alice grew resentful and by the time Christian went to university, they hardly saw each other. It was only when Alice had gone away to art college that the siblings messaged each other more frequently and arranged regular get-togethers.

She had loved having her brother back again. But learning the lesson of her childhood, she had kept communication minimal but regular, figuring that Christian would up the amount of contact when he was ready. She had thought it was all going so well. And now she had blown it.

There was only one thing for it. Alice took out the special CD she kept for these occasions. She turned up the volume and danced around the saloon to 'Spice Up Your Life'. When she felt her life had been spiced enough, she combed through the kitchen cupboards and found a bottle of wine left over from Christian's dinner. She poured a glass and took a large gulp.

Alice checked her bank account for Eleanor's upfront fee. As a new business, she had little cashflow and the advance was supposed to cover any expenses she incurred. But the money was not there. Alice tutted aloud. She drafted a chasing email, but she was loathe to pester her new client for money so soon, so she deleted it. Her business bank account was in the red. She checked her personal account. The same story there.

"Anyone home?"

"Come in, Roddy. There's wine on the counter if you'd like a glass."

"I most certainly would." Roddy helped himself and eased into a seat. He gave a long sigh as he crossed one ankle over his knee, flip-flop dropping to the floor. "And what has the Alice Haydon curatorial service been up to today?"

"Making lists of all the crap in the Carberrys' drawers," Alice said glowering at her laptop.

"That doesn't sound very glamorous."

Alice looked up. "There's just so much stuff. Eleanor's grandfather was a prodigious collector of, well, you name it – guns, stones, dead insects with pins through them and much more."

"Anything interesting?"

"Actually, yes. Wilfred was a decent artist and there are sketchbooks full of lovely drawings. Anyway, enough of me. What have you been up to?"

"Helping your brother move into The Bull."

So, Christian really had left. Alice felt her eyes well and she clutched the coffee table. Christian gone already and he had only just arrived …

"Dear girl, are you alright?"

"Christian's left."

Roddy knelt beside her and put an arm across her shoulder. His touch brought tears to her cheeks and she sobbed into Roddy's chest.

"I'm sure it's only temporary." Roddy stroked the back of Alice's head. "He wants to be near Devi, so it's understandable that he'd rather stay at the hotel."

Alice wiped her cheeks with the back of her hand. "No, that's not it. He moved out because I told him his relationship with Devi wouldn't go anywhere. He was angry with me."

"I expect he saw it as his pesky little sister interfering in his love life. But Christian's a big boy and he'll get over it. Give it a couple of days, then pop over and see how he is. I'm sure he'll be glad you did. He's very fond of you, you know."

"I suppose." Alice breathed deep and dug for a smile. "Let's talk about something else. How's the exhibition shaping up?"

"Productively. I've done some sketches of Renton Hall's grounds which, by the way, I thoroughly enjoyed strolling around." Roddy sat back on the floor.

"That's … What did you do to your leg? That's a nasty cut."

Roddy brushed the angry red line on his calf. "I caught something sharp when I was following a blond-haired man through the woods."

Alice's felt her stomach knot. "You found him."

"I thought I did. I was ambling through the woods wondering why there were so many dead trees, when I saw a mop of blond hair amongst the foliage. So I chased him."

Alice's mouth dropped open. "You chased him?"

"I did. And then I snagged my leg. While I was extracting myself from the undergrowth, blondie vanished."

"How very interesting. It has to be the same man who spoke to Nick at the party. I wonder who he is?"

Roddy twirled a strand of beard. "I've made it my mission to find out."

"Let's hope that's soon. I feel like we're treading water."

Alice looked over Roddy's shoulder and out to the river. Flashes of the Great Wheaton Rowing Club's colours dashed by. Droplets slid down the window as grey clouds darkened the landscape. Alice's own landscape was becoming blurry too.

"Well, look on the bright side," said Roddy. "It can't get any worse."

"Yes, it can. I'm broke."

Chapter 13

THE NEXT MORNING, ALICE boarded a train at Great Wheaton station, her straitened financial situation heavy on her mind. Eleanor's upfront fee would have covered the cost of this trip to pick up a Carberry painting from Cheryl Horton. With both business and personal bank accounts empty, Alice did not have enough for the fare to London. Asking Joe to lend her money would have been to admit that she could not manage her finances. Instead, she lifted a few notes from the emergency cash supply Joe kept in an empty coffee tin. Now wracked with guilt, she willed herself to come up with a plan to pay back the money before Joe noticed it was missing.

Alice could not invoice Emilio Gambi until the photographs were hung, although she had already paid for the framing. She regretted agreeing to that arrangement – she should have insisted on Emilio paying for the framing in advance.

Emilio was emphatic that the photograph of Nonno in his restaurant in Italy should form the centrepiece of the display in his own eatery. He would not be talked out of it, despite the sorry state of the picture. Alice did not have high hopes for it, but she had left it in the capable hands of Terry the framer to come up with a solution. But now she was having second thoughts. What if he experimented and caused even more damage? If it all went wrong, she would have to pay for it herself. Another financial headache!

The train pulled into King's Cross. Alice left her anxieties in the carriage and made her way to the underground. She was meeting Cheryl at her office in Soho, but there was an hour to kill before then. She stepped out of the lift at Covent Garden for a spot of pre-meeting shopping; that is, window shopping.

Alice put on sunglasses as she crossed the cobbled piazza. A man seated on an upturned crate strummed a guitar as a woman in a flowy red dress danced. A crowd gathered in a semi-circle around them. Children sat on the edge of Central Market, peering up at a top-hatted man on stilts, who was pulling paper roses from his sleeve.

Alice ambled by the shops underneath the glass-domed roof. Knowing she could not afford to buy anything put a new spin on shopping. She spotted a window filled with the new range of Vans. Nose to the glass, Alice took in this season's colours and styles; with a full purse she could have bought any pair. Instead, she looked down at the ones she was wearing, black with white soles, and convinced herself they were the most attractive pair. Alice put one in front of the other and headed for Soho.

Alice was buzzed into a building with a bright green door and found Cheryl waiting for her at the top of a steep flight of steps. Behind her was the open door to a photographer's studio. Two lights on tripods beamed down on a blue-haired woman lying on a polished wooden floor. A young man fiddled with a white screen behind her, while the photographer appeared to be clicking through the model's previous shots.

Cheryl led Alice around the studio and into a small room with one tiny window. Boxes were stacked high against a wall; shots of women in swimwear were taped to another. A computer screen with post-it notes stuck down one side filled a tiny desk in the corner.

"Excuse the mess, there's not much room." Cheryl moved an armful of bikinis from a director's chair. "But Katie's a friend and as she takes my photos, she doesn't charge much for the office."

Alice picked up a catalogue, a photo of a smiling Cheryl wearing a one-shouldered orange swimsuit on the cover. "So, you design the collection and model the clothes yourself?"

"Yes. As I always tell people, I'm a one-woman show." Cheryl crossed a toned, tanned leg over the other.

Alice flicked through the glossy pages. Cheryl paddling in the sea, draped alluringly on a diving board and swinging off ropes on a yacht. Keeping those washboard abs must be a full-time job!

"We shot that collection in Antigua, which was fab. That's the great thing about this job, I get to choose the locations."

There were no prices in the catalogue, so Alice had to ask.

"The bikinis average around a hundred and twenty pounds, the one-pieces are a bit more."

Alice gulped. "I suppose that's the going rate for designer swimwear …"

"Believe it or not, I'm undercutting the competition at those prices. But the shoots are expensive and you can't skimp on those."

In the harsh overhead light and with her long hair pulled back into a ponytail, Cheryl looked all of her forty-four years. Wrinkles creased her forehead and a deep frown line cut down between her eyes. Her pale skin was blotched and listless. But beneath her unbuttoned shirt, there was no denying she had a very good bosom.

"Well, you're close to the heart of the rag trade here, so there's plenty of outlets to sell your lines."

"But every man and his dog are flogging their ranges. I'm not going to lie Alice, it's tough out there. I haven't got a taker for my winter collection yet."

"Katie!" a man yelled from the studio. "Here a minute."

Cheryl smiled. "It does get a bit noisy here sometimes. Let's go to the café next door, we can talk properly there."

"I'll take Eleanor's painting with me now, otherwise I'll forget it," said Alice.

Cheryl had borrowed the piece from Renton Hall to use as a prop for one of her shoots and Eleanor has asked Alice to collect it for her.

"Did you use the painting?"

"Absolutely. Me and Katie put together a living room set here in the studio and I needed something for the wall. The pics are here somewhere." Cheryl rummaged around her desk and produced sheets of proofs. Cheryl dressed in floaty maxi dresses, sprawled on a sofa, or leaning against a bookcase watching television.

"I thought I'd branch out, so I designed a line of evening dresses. Originally, I was going to sell them as part of my cruise collection. In the end I thought they'd work as anytime dresses, so I was going for a homely setting in the promotional literature. But now I've seen the shots, I'm not sure ..." Cheryl gave a wry smile and tossed the proofs on the desk. "Back to the swimming pool, I think."

Cheryl ordered coffee and cinnamon rolls and the two women sat on wooden benches beside the window.

"This is my favourite seat. I can see the world walk by," said Cheryl. "It gets a bit lonely in the office at times."

Alice bit into the sticky bun, delighted at its soft, chewy texture and generous proportions.

"How's things at Renton Hall?" said Cheryl.

"I'm working my way through the attic, though it's a much bigger inventory than I anticipated. When I say there's stuff everywhere, I mean literally everywhere."

"That's what Harry said. He and Nick used to hide up there as children, so he's pulled out every drawer and opened every box in his time."

"I may need to call on his memory if I run out of time."

Cheryl walked fingers around her bun, but it remained untouched. "And what about the interior decorator? I get the impression that Eleanor is terrified of her."

"Gina's a bit scary. I've looked up her previous projects and she's worked for celebrities and even royalty. I'm sure the hotel will be fabulous when it's finished."

"Let's hope no more dead bodies turn up, then. All this bad publicity will kill the hotel before it opens."

Cheryl's phone buzzed. She checked the caller, then put the phone on silent. As she did so, Alice pondered a question that had been on her mind all morning. The Jamaican invoices that Harry had referred to in The Bull – Alice could not see how they had anything to do with

Nick Carberry's death, but she had to know for sure. So she asked Cheryl about them.

"I'm not sure exactly," said Cheryl. "Some irregularity with the accounting, something like that. I don't know the details."

"Perhaps I should ask Harry as it was he who mentioned it."

"No!" Cheryl gripped Alice's arm. "Please don't." She let go and gave a half-smile. "Sorry. I just meant that you shouldn't pester Harry, he has enough to worry about. And any mention of the agency would only upset him."

Alice watched a mother drag a crying child into the next booth. But at the corner of her eye she caught Cheryl blowing out a breath.

"So where are you going for your next shoot?" said Alice. "Somewhere exotic?"

"If only. The way my finances are at the moment, I'm not sure I can afford another shoot just now."

"I know the feeling. It's my first foray into running my own business and keeping on top of my finances is a permanent worry."

"And it doesn't get any easier. I've had my business for seven years and it's even harder now than it was at the beginning."

"Oh dear, that's not very encouraging."

"Sorry, but don't let me put you off. You're probably better at keeping track of what you spend, I'm just hopeless with money. Honestly, I don't know where it goes."

"What about Harry? Does he help at all?"

"God no, he's not interested in the swimwear business. Which is just as well as he'd freak out if he knew how much money I'd borrowed."

Like Alice, Cheryl had not turned to her partner to bail her company out. But by trying to prove she could be successful on her own, perhaps Cheryl had allowed her business to pay the price.

"So, it's all down to Renton Hall now," said Cheryl. "If the hotel doesn't make money, I'm stuffed."

"I didn't realise you had a stake in the project. I thought the Hall belonged to Eleanor and Nick."

"Oh, I don't have a share. I mean, not directly. It's Harry – he does."

"I'm sorry, I must have misunderstood. I was sure Eleanor said that her mother gave up her own interest in the house and passed it to her children."

"Well, that's true. But now that Nick's dead, his share will be passed on. Nick always said that he'd make sure Harry was looked after if anything should happen to him. Harry will inherit Nick's share of Renton Hall."

Alice stared at Cheryl's uplifted chin. The revelation that she would be in the money again had taken years off Cheryl. Now the image of her toned body in skimpy, neon bikinis was not such a stretch.

"Harry's not interested in the decorating part, he's left all that to Eleanor. But I've got a few design ideas of my own, which are just what the old building needs. And I intend to give that Gina a piece of my mind."

Chapter 14

ALICE WAS PLEASED TO have *Daisy* to herself. She needed to take stock. Picking a cough candy out of her sweet jar, Alice grabbed a box of push pins. She sat cross-legged on the beanbag and wedged the edge of her incident board underneath it while she added new information. Alongside the pictures of Simon Newgate and Harry Horton she pinned one of Cheryl. As she would indirectly benefit from Nick's death, Cheryl had to be a suspect. And that made three. Nick's business partner, his cousin and his cousin's wife.

Had Nick ever suspected that he was surrounded by so many people with a credible motive to get rid of him? Alice was just about to pin up another picture when Roddy opened the hatch door.

"You don't mind me joining you do you? I need a break."

"Of course not, come on in."

"I'm delighted to announce that I've finished one of my landscapes. I sat on my deck in the sunshine and whipped up a watercolour." Roddy put his hands on his hips. "And it's not half bad."

"Wonderful! You must be relieved to have a finished piece under your belt."

"I am. I'd forgotten that when I pulled exhibitions together before, I always had a few paintings to start off with. But doing an entire show from scratch is playing havoc with my nerves." Roddy flopped onto the sofa, hands behind his head.

"It's exciting too," said Alice. "The gallery usually puts on a good opening. The press will be there and lots of guests and you'll have to make a speech. You must be looking forward to it."

"I thought I was passed all that razzmatazz, but I do get a few flutters whenever I think of it. How are things at the Hall?"

"Trying!

"Your life can't always be as exciting as mine, Alice! Still, you're getting paid to do the inventory, which should keep your business going."

"Except it's not. Eleanor is a slow payer, or more accurately, a no-payer. And I've had to fork out for Emilio's framing work, so I've got a cashflow problem."

"No money, eh? That's clients for you. But Eleanor's a decent sort, she'll pay up soon I'm sure. So, apart from your money issues, are you enjoying running your own company?"

"I'm loving it. Not having a boss telling me what to do is heaven. And being able to work from *Daisy* is a special bonus."

"You don't miss your colleagues? It can get a bit lonely working by yourself."

"I haven't had time to be lonely. Apart from the work, there's the strange case of Nick Carberry to occupy us."

Roddy looked at the incident board. "Another suspect I see. Do you think one of them is a stronger suspect than the others?"

"Not really. To be honest, they all have similar motives: money and jealousy. They all knew Nick well and had easy access to him at the party."

"I haven't heard any news from the police, so I'm assuming that means they don't have a prime suspect either."

"Apparently not, though I'm going to the station soon to give a statement. Which I should have done by now. Anyway, I'll find out more then. Frankly, I'm stumped on this case and a killer on the loose at Renton Hall in starting to freak me out. Especially since you told me about the mystery blond in the woods. Have you found out anything more on that?"

"I tried my most reliable source first, and—"

"Stanley?"

"Stanley. He knew Eleanor's father George, and he reminded me that I had met him myself. Stanley and I were at The Bull one evening and George came in for a quick drink. We chatted for a bit, then someone suggested we play cards, so we spent the rest of the evening playing poker."

"I didn't know you played."

"I don't. Unfortunately, George did. Very well. Which is how he ended up with one of my paintings. I lost all the cash I had on me, and in a rash moment I bet my most expensive piece on what I thought was a good hand."

Alice snorted. "That's hilarious. But wait a minute, I haven't seen it at the Hall. And I don't mean to give you a big head, but that would be one of the better pieces."

Roddy twirled a strand of grey beard. "George did say the painting wasn't to his wife's taste when he picked it up from my studio. I'm not convinced it was to his own taste either. He probably sold it on."

"Well, it doesn't help us with the case."

"No. Though I do remember George talking about his own father's artistic endeavours. He particularly liked Wilfred's work. Though he didn't seem fond of the man himself."

"Really? And yet Eleanor seems to worship Wilfred."

"George was his son and I did detect some rivalry between the two of them. Or rather that George felt he could never do anything to please his father. But he also said that Wilfred wasn't the saint people thought he was."

"Did he say why?"

"We were sampling the establishment's good wines and this was later on in the evening ... But, he said something like, 'Wilfred could be paid to keep his mouth shut.' Or, 'Wilfred kept secrets for cash.' The exact words won't come now but I remember being struck with George's disdain for his father, even at the time."

"Well, that's helpful background."

Roddy went over to Alice's board and picked up a photograph from the floor. "A dog? If you're suggesting that a canine is amongst the suspects, then we're in serious trouble!"

"Not a suspect, but a possible motive. Nick Carberry was killed over a dog. Or so Sarah Evans seems to think."

"I've always said that dog owners are mad!" Roddy laughed. "She can't be serious?"

Alice took the picture of Wilson from Roddy. "Deadly, it would appear. I've no idea what she means and this is the only dog I've seen around Renton Hall. Though I find it hard to believe that this little fella was the cause of a fatal dispute."

"Believe it. Somebody once threatened to kill me over a pineapple!" Roddy waved a finger at Alice. "Don't ask.

Though in my defence, we had started by arguing about a woman!"

"That I *can* believe."

Roddy pointed at a second picture. "Jeremy Evans?"

"His murder is a bigger mystery than Nick's. According to Eleanor, he was Mr Congeniality. So why would anyone want to kill him?"

"Oh, there is a reason. We just have to find out what it is."

Alice sat in Great Wheaton Police Station's interview room, staring at a grey wall, as she had done for the past fifteen minutes. A long time to stare at a grey wall. When she had arrived to give her statement, she was ushered into the room, invited to sit on an uncomfortable plastic chair and told to wait.

With no windows and a shut door, the walls closed in. Alice paced around the room. Four strides across the width. Four down the length. Moisture gathered at her throat and she pulled at the neck of her t-shirt. After what seemed ages but was probably only two minutes, the door clicked open. DI Nathan Salisbury strode in.

Nathan sat opposite Alice, hands on the table, palms down. His broad shoulders were hunched over and a cloud shadowed his handsome face. "I wanted to have a quiet word with you, Alice, before DS Riley comes in to take your full statement."

Heat rushed to Alice's cheeks. She patted a palm on one side of her face, as if to push the heat back inside.

Nathan looked over Alice's shoulder. "I know you've had a preliminary interview with DS Riley. Thank you for answering his questions. There are a couple of points

I want to clarify with you. Firstly, let's go back to when you discovered Jeremy Evans in the hayloft." Nathan's grey eyes darkened. "You said that you went into the downstairs area of Mr Evans' house. You were looking for some sculptures. Is that correct?"

"Yes." Alice's voice cracked. "Yes. Eleanor Carberry told me that Jeremy, that is Mr Evans, had found some ceramics in his snug and she wanted me to have a look at them."

"So, you were in Mr Evans' snug because Eleanor Carberry had asked you to look at some ceramics?"

"That's correct."

"And there was nobody else in the building when you got there?"

"No."

"Or while you were there? You didn't see anybody else at all?"

Alice shuffled on her seat. "No."

"And what about outside the building? Did you see anybody in the fields as you walked from Renton Hall? Or in the wooded area?"

Alice went back to Tuesday afternoon and pictured herself as she left the conservatory. She walked over the little bridge and alongside the paddock. She would have easily spotted someone across the open landscape, but the nearest she had seen to a person was Nick's sculpture on the decking. She had not seen or heard anybody, though it would have been easy enough for somebody to remain hidden in the wood.

"No. I didn't see anybody else from the time I left the Hall, until I saw Mr Evans."

"Thank you. Now if I could take you back to when you discovered Mr Evans. You told DS Riley that you wanted to have a nose around the hayloft. Earlier, you had seen some old furniture that was being readied for auction and you wanted to have a proper look. Is that correct?"

"Yes, that's right. I … yes."

Nathan smiled. Was he trying to reassure her? "And when you found Mr Evans, you were alone?"

"Yes."

Nathan formed a steeple with his fingers and tapped it against his nose. He looked down at the table for a moment, then he fixed his eyes on Alice's.

"We found the gun used to shoot Mr Evans. It was an old service revolver, part of the gun collection kept in Renton Hall's attic." Nathan linked his hands. "Luckily, we found a clear fingerprint on the grip, which we have been able to identify. So we now have a suspect for Mr Evans' murder."

Alice wondered which of the suspects it was. Simon Newgate, Harry Horton or Cheryl Horton?

"You. The fingerprint on the gun, Alice, is yours."

Chapter 15

Livvie Manners unwrapped a double chocolate brownie and handed it to Alice. "You said it was an emergency and that means brownies, right?"

"Not that sort of emergency," Alice said sitting up on the sun lounger on *Daisy*'s deck.

Alice could not get Nathan Salisbury's face out of her mind. Once Nathan had told her that her fingerprints were on the gun, Alice had not heard another word he said. Though she did notice his serious expression. She was aware of him helping her up and guiding her out the door. She knew that he had handed her a card. The rest was a blur.

As she walked back to *Daisy,* Alice pictured the gun collection in the attic at Renton Hall. She watched the glass shelf crash, she saw herself collecting the pieces from the floor. And then she remembered picking up the service revolver.

She, of all people, should have known better. Art and antique collections often contain fragile or priceless pieces. And handling, or even touching them could cause irreparable damage. All Alice's training and experience screamed that she should not have touched anything without protective gloves and the utmost care. In this case though, far from damaging the gun, she had damaged herself. She was a murder suspect.

Alice closed her eyes and flopped back on the lounger.

"Okay, so … a different sort of emergency." Livvie rustled through her canvas bag. "Let's see, you call me at the café, tell me to come over immediately and then you just sit there and don't tell me what's happened. No really, it's fine. I'll just guess."

Alice opened her eyes. Livvie was holding a small bottle of whisky. "This sort of emergency?"

Alice nodded. Livvie poured a measure into Alice's coffee. "There you go."

Alice sipped her drink. An instant hit from the water of life cleared her head.

"Feel better?"

"Thanks Livvie, that was just what I needed."

"So, are you going to tell me what's going on? You're starting to scare me."

Alice told Livvie about her meeting with Nathan.

"But he doesn't suspect you, right? Nathan knows that you just touched the thing by accident. I mean you picked up loads of pieces, right?"

"Yes. No. Actually I'm not sure. I think he believed me. But he also said he had to corroborate my story." Alice put both hands around the mug. "Though I don't know how, there was nobody else in the attic at the time."

"Nathan's a smart man and he knows you Alice. Having a former boyfriend who still holds a torch for you, well that's got to count for something."

"Nathan will be his usual diligent self. He won't jeopardise the investigation because of his feelings for me. Which, by the way, are not what you think they are. Nathan and I split up years ago."

"Okay, you think what you want, but that man still has the hots for you." Livvie shielded her eyes with her hand.

"Like me or not, Nathan has me down as a suspect until he can prove that I didn't kill Jeremy Evans."

"Nathan will quickly eliminate you from his incident board; meantime, you should find out who the real killer is. My customers at The Coffee Pot can't talk about anything else."

"One of three people killed Nick Carberry and Jeremy Evans. Though I'm not sure I understand why."

If Jeremy Evans' widow was right, the only unexplored motive for the murders, unlikely as it seemed to Alice, was Eleanor's Yorkshire terrier. Alice had to find out why the dog was so important. And fast.

Alice found Sarah Evans in her garden, picking strawberries. She popped one in her mouth before dropping another into a basket, taking off her gloves and shoving them into her trouser pocket.

In the kitchen, a large pot bubbled on the hob, steaming the windows despite the open back door. Sarah made a pot of tea and carried it out to a bench in the garden.

"So, you've come about the dog," said Sarah. "I suspected you might, though I've not much more to tell you. Jeremy said it was just an ordinary statue and he couldn't see what all the fuss was about."

"A statue? So it's not a real dog?"

"Heavens no." Sarah cracked a smile. "And there you were, thinking I was talking about a real animal. No, it's one of those ornamental things that people put in their gardens. Can't see the point of them myself, but Jeremy said he was very attached to it."

"He? By which you mean Nick Carberry?"

"Oh no, the man next door. Bill Trevelyan. It was his dog."

So, Nick Carberry had argued with somebody over a statue of a dog?

"Are you sure, Sarah? I don't mean to be dismissive, but I'm finding it hard to understand why Nick could fall out with someone over something so … ordinary. Why the dog would be the cause of two deaths."

"Well as they so wisely say, there's none as queer as folk."

"Indeed. So who was doing the arguing? I'm assuming that both Nick Carberry and Jeremy were involved?"

"Nick was most upset about it. Got quite agitated, so Jeremy told me. But goodness, what is the point of getting in a state over a silly statue. And Nick was always such a sensible boy."

"Have you seen this dog yourself?"

"No. Jeremy said it was nothing special and not worth a visit."

Special or not, Alice had to see it for herself.

WAITING AT NAREBRIDGE ROAD T-junction, Alice glimpsed her brother. Christian was in the back of a taxi chatting to Devi. Alice's heart skipped. She had not heard from Christian since he had left *Daisy*. Reluctantly agreeing with Roddy that she should give him time to calm down, she had not contacted him. She hoped that he would get in touch when he was ready. But he was clearly not ready yet. And Alice was missing him.

She debated whether to give him a call. She did not want to pester him and if he ignored her call, she would be hurt. On the other hand, Christian himself might be upset if she did not at least try to make contact. Brothers were complicated creatures!

At Renton Hall, the decorators had moved their paraphernalia into the sitting room and were painting the walls lemon. The colour lifted the dimmest and least attractive of the downstairs rooms. But Alice had a dog to find, so she walked over the bridge and up the track beside the wood to find the dog statue. At Jeremy's snug, she followed the path into the wood.

Sunbeams flashed between branches of soaring trees, flaming the leaves. Underfoot, the narrow path was carpeted with vegetation damp from the night's rain. Alice slipped a couple of times, her fashionable Vans not designed for rural conditions. She was through the woods sooner than she expected and found herself standing in a field. A large farmhouse stood about fifty metres away. Bill Trevelyan's home.

A Land Rover was parked beside the front door. In the centre of the turning circle, water spouted from a silver dolphin in an elaborate stone fountain. A gravel driveway, with several potholes, led down to the main road. There was no ornamental dog.

It was likely to be in the back garden, so keeping close to the wood, Alice tracked left. A high, raggedy privet hedge ran from the edge of the house, separating a paddock from what Alice assumed to be a private family garden. Walking across the exposed paddock would be risky; she might be seen from one of the house windows. She shaded her eyes with both hands, but could see no movement. Taking a chance, she jogged across the grass.

At the house, she put her back to the brickwork and peered around the corner. All clear. She crept along the towering privet hedge, until she reached a patch of thinning shrubs. Finding a gap, she peered through. Four square flowerbeds were separated by a gravel path in the shape of a cross. Rampant bushes of rosemary and mint scented the sultry air. Fingers of peas and plump tomatoes ripened on the vine.

A woman with a scarf tied under her chin knelt at one of the squares. Digging out potatoes with a trowel, she brushed off the earth with gardening gloves that almost reached her elbows, and threw the vegetables into a wheelbarrow. Mrs Trevelyan, presumably.

Alice scanned the kitchen garden, but there were no dogs, ornamental or otherwise. She turned back again and checking that the woman was occupied, she crept to the corner of the privet hedge, jogged back across the grass and into the trees.

Now in a different part of the wood, Alice walked straight through assuming that she would still end up back on the Renton Hall estate. She found a path by a holly bush. Treetops met and the wood darkened as Alice picked her way along the path until it disappeared. She pushed a branch away from her face and climbed over an uprooted tree trunk. Alice stopped and peered through the bushes, but could see nothing other than more vegetation.

The wood grew gloomy but Alice pressed on. She stubbed her toe on a plank, hobbled to one side, tripped over a wire and fell to her knees. She put one foot on the ground and held onto a large stone to lever herself up. She rubbed her hands and as she bent down to brush the earth from her trousers, she noticed the markings on the stone.

Alice took out her phone and switched on the torch. She ran the beam across the engraving and made out the words, 'Charlie 1984–1990'. A headstone! There was another one next to it, this one reading, 'Felix 1976–1980'. Gosh, some poor woman had buried two children. A rustle from the bush behind her made Alice spin around. She moved the torch from side to side but could see nothing other than foliage.

Not wishing to go back the way she had come and risk tripping on the wire again, she edged around the two headstones. On the other side was a wrought iron bench with ivy growing along one armrest. And lying on the seat was a cat. Alice hesitated. The cat did not move. Alice shone her torch in its face and when it still did not move, she bent down to touch it. It was made of stone.

On the ground beside the bench was a greyhound, sitting straight and tall and staring with sightless eyes into the gloom. Two animals on the edge of a cemetery? It must be a pet cemetery!

Alice patted the greyhound's head. "And you, my friend, must be the stone dog."

Chapter 16

TWO MEN WERE DEAD over a statue of a dog. Alice was no nearer to understanding why, even after seeing it. A stone dog, in a pet cemetery, in a wood. It did not look as if anyone had visited the site for years. Why would anybody care about it?

Alice manoeuvred the Defender into a tight spot on Great Wheaton high street and began walking. The Town Hall clock struck five, so she picked up speed and darted into the framer's shop.

Terry Conrad had begun his working life as a carpenter until he realised he could make more money, more easily, with a framing service. He had opened his shop thirty years ago, framing expensive paintings, school photographs and amateur watercolours for local residents. Alice supposed that Terry could tell a lot about people from the images they brought him and she wondered what he thought about Emilio Gambi.

"That's a fine collection of photographs." Terry rubbed his stubbly chin. "I haven't framed a family of Italian pizza makers before. They're a good looking lot, especially that Dean Martin. What relation is he?"

"He's an imaginary cousin! I'm not sure how he got there, but I'm told he's a permanent part of the collection."

Terry's smile was wide enough to reveal a gap where a molar should be. "Well they're all done for you. It's at the higher rate, if that's okay, since you needed them done quickly."

Bandy legs took Terry to a back room and he returned with two of the pictures. One was a black and white photograph of Emilio with two young boys. An ivory mount with a thin red frame complemented the smiling family.

"Fantastic," said Alice. "I'm really pleased with that. How did you get on with the others?"

Terry turned towards the window and the light caught a diamond in his ear. "All good, expect for the really old one."

"Yes, Nonno's picture is the one I was worried about. How did it work out?"

Terry handed over the second picture. "See for yourself."

This photo was smaller than the previous one. It was double mounted and had the same red frame. Nonno Gambi was laughing as he shook the mayor's hand. The photo looked clearer than Alice remembered.

"This is terrific, Terry. You've cut off the damaged bottom section, but you don't notice that this photo is smaller than the others because the double mount gives it more body. In fact, it will stand out on the wall, which is exactly what Emilio wanted. That's clever." Alice lifted the image closer. "But you've done something to the surface. It looks newer. What is it?"

Terry tapped the side of his nose. "Terry's secret." He laughed. "Glad you like it."

"Emilio will be delighted."

"It's Sunday, the opening, isn't it?"

"Yes, so I'll be hanging these tomorrow."

Terry took the photo back. "I'll get them wrapped up and delivered to Emilio's first thing."

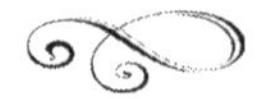

Alice opened *Daisy*'s hatch door, turned on the deck light and leaned over the barge's side. A demure moon cast shimmering lines across the river, broken by Mr and Mrs Swan gliding towards their nest on the old wooden jetty. Opposite, cows packed together underneath the big oak tree, water caressing the bank beneath them. An owl hooted from the barn at the riding stables behind.

Alice closed her eyes and breathed deeply. She lifted up her face and a cool breeze stroked her cheeks. Opening her arms wide, she stretched to the tip of her fingers.

Thump! The deck vibrated under Alice's feet.

"I'm so sorry," said Roddy. "Am I interrupting some kind of moon worship?"

"I was just having a quiet moment." Alice folded her arms. "It's been a long day."

"Then it's a good job I brought this." Roddy presented a bottle of wine. He poured two glasses and sat on a director's chair, crossing an ankle over his knee. "Now tell me the gossip. What's the latest with Christian and Devi?"

"I saw them today as they shot passed me in a taxi. But apart from that, I've no idea. I haven't heard from Christian."

Roddy twirled a strand of grey beard. "He's probably calmed down now, so you could contact him and see how he is."

"I thought I would ask him and Devi to lunch with me and Joe on Sunday. It's Emilio's opening and he's offering free pizza."

"Dear girl, you're going to invite your brother to a free pizza lunch? That wasn't what I had in mind for a patch-up session."

"Emilio's expecting a big turnout and I thought it would be less awkward to be in a crowd, instead of having a proper sit-down lunch. No pressure on Christian to talk if he doesn't want to."

"I stand corrected." Roddy winked. "Rather thoughtful in fact."

"Do you think he'll come? I'll be gutted if he doesn't."

"Of course he will. After all, it is free pizza!"

"You sneer, but Emilio's pizzas will be amazing. I've heard all about the secret family recipe and it involves some very special tomatoes!"

"You know, I might saunter down myself if there's free food. I can't remember the last time I ate pizza. Now, tell me …" Roddy sauntered across the deck and leant against the side. "How's your part of the investigation going?"

"Still the same three suspects. The only wrinkle is that I had assumed the same person killed both Nick Carberry and Jeremy Evans. But I can't see a connection between them, so now, I'm not so sure."

"And the dog?"

"Don't ask! To be honest, the whole thing is more baffling now than when I started."

"Tell me what you know about it. I'm intrigued."

"Sarah Evans said that Nick Carberry got agitated about a dog statue. And she didn't know any more than that. Bizarre really."

"It must be a very special statue."

"You would think. But I've found it and it's nothing special. I was in the wood that divides the Renton Hall estate from its neighbour, and I stumbled across a pet cemetery."

Roddy screwed up his face. "How macabre. Bury the beasts, yes, but headstones and statues?"

"Anyway, sitting on the edge was a rather ugly stone statue of a greyhound. It has to be Sarah's dog."

"But stuck in the middle of a wood? How would that bother anybody?" Roddy refilled their glasses.

"I suppose that was the point, to keep it out of the way," said Alice. "Though I expect it kept the Carberry children occupied for a while. Perhaps the cemetery was created specially for them – a place to visit their beloved pets. Perhaps it only become neglected when they grew up and lost interest."

"It belongs to the Carberrys then?"

"I just assumed it belonged to them. The wood marks the boundary between the Carberrys and their neighbours. But I don't know exactly where one property ends and the other begins."

"So, it could be the neighbour's?"

Alice had not considered that the pet cemetery might belonged to the Trevelyans. "Roddy, help me out for a moment. If the cemetery and dog belong to the Trevelyans, in what circumstances could it possibly have upset Nick Carberry? It's tucked away out of sight. And when I was there today, I didn't see anything to upset anybody." Alice pursed her lips. "Except for the dead animals, of course."

"Dear girl, this has got to be the strangest conversation we've ever had. Or have I drunk too much wine?"

"I told you it was baffling." Alice laughed. "Though I do wonder whether this pet cemetery, macabre as it is, holds the key. As there isn't an obvious line between the two properties, perhaps there was an argument about that. Or maybe it really is about the dog. Somebody stole somebody else's dog. Or something?"

"I'm beginning to lose the will to live ... Though I think your boundary idea may have some merit," said Roddy. "Talking of Trevelyan, I was in The Coffee Pot today and I got chatting to Mikey Case. He told me an interesting story about Mr Bill Trevelyan."

"Mikey Case?"

"The man who lives on *Peppermint*. The barge four in front of Daisy."

"Oh, I thought his name was Jim. I've always called him Jim."

"Dear girl!"

"Anyway, what did he say?"

Roddy looked over his shoulder. "Well, it seems that the Carberry's respectable neighbour is something of a dark horse. In his younger days he had a string of affairs. One mistress after another, so Mikey said."

"What a pair of gossips you two are! Interesting stuff, though! How would Bill have got away with it for so long? His wife must have found out, surely?"

"It sounds as though Trevelyan tried to be discreet. But he had staff and everyone knew him. And this—"

"Is a small town. Yes, I know." Alice looked over the darkened river.

"Before we leave the Carberrys, may I ask whether Eleanor has paid up yet?"

"No! I was going to chase it up today, but I didn't see her. It's not the sort of conversation I want to have over the phone."

"But she does owe you the money and it's not out of order for you to remind her."

Alice did not want to discuss money with Roddy. Whilst she appreciated his support and guidance, he did not have to know every detail of her life. And she was not going to give him, or anyone else for that matter, the lowdown on her hopeless financial situation.

"If you could continue your enquiries, Roddy, I would be grateful. Perhaps Mikey has some more gossip that might shed a light on Nick's murder."

"Don't underestimate the power of the chattering class. Though of course, I have far better sources than Mikey." Roddy raised his chin. "On other matters, how is Joe? I haven't seen him for a while."

"He's fine. Very busy as always, he's been working away a lot recently."

"Which means you can spend time on *Daisy*. You must be glad you decided to keep her."

"One of the best decisions I've made for ages. Though the owners are due back next year when their contract in Singapore is up. And I'm already panicking about losing *Daisy.*"

Daisy had never let Alice down. Everything about her felt right – her cosy saloon with Alice's favourite paintings on the walls, her deck for relaxed socialising, her reassuring, somehow timeless bulk. Alice did not know how she would be able to give her back to the owners.

Roddy twirled the empty wine glass in his hand. "I was going to suggest a spot of supper. But I've got no food on board and I'm guessing you don't either. How do you fancy a quick bite at Livvie's?"

Chapter 17

SWELLING CLOUDS HUNG OVER the river, a whippy wind buffeting the Great Wheaton Rowing Club flag, but that did not discourage the team. Eight teenage girls in club vests pushed away from the bank and eased into matching strokes, encouraged by their shouty cox. Brawling ducks gobbled Sunday morning breakfast from little hands spraying chunks of bread across the water. Couples cradled takeaway coffees and dogs pulled on leads, anticipating a romp through the fields.

Two floors up on Joe's balcony, Alice watched Simon Newgate wander along the riverside path. He was wearing a white baseball cap, but Alice caught his face when he stopped to chat to a man pushing a pram.

It seemed ages since Alice had met Simon in his office. The meeting had come directly after Eleanor's insistence that Simon was Nick Carberry's killer. Had Eleanor's words coloured Alice's judgement of Nick's business partner? But if Simon Newgate was a suspect, where did the stone dog fit in? Had Simon bought it? Or perhaps he had designed it? Was it was modelled on a real dog? Simon's dog?

So many questions, but there was one immediate question to answer. What should she wear for lunch?

The queue snaked away from the entrance to Emilio's Pizza Parlour and along the high street. The promise of free food was clearly a draw, but the smell of fresh basil and rich tomato sauce must have contributed to the growing crowd.

Emilio Gambi was at the door greeting people, as Alice and Joe arrived. He directed new arrivals to the back of the queue, expressing sympathy for the wait. "What can I do?" he said. "Everybody wants to eat Emilio's special pizzas."

When Emilio spotted Alice, he waved her through the door. "I can't have my special guests kept waiting." He kissed her on both cheeks. "Go on in. Antonia will look after you." He yelled inside, "Antonia! Alice is here."

A round woman with a dark messy bun and a warm smile, threw her arms around Alice and patted her back. "We love the photos, Alice. Your frames make them look special. Nonno would be very proud." Antonia embraced Joe. "Come on in and have some food." Antonia took Alice's hand and pulled her through the crowd of people cradling slices of pizza on little sheets of greaseproof paper.

"Lot of customers. Emilio's will be very popular I think. We even have a movie star here. Yes, a real one, all the way from India. I introduce you."

With her wavy hair cascading over her shoulders, Devi looked every inch the movie star. Alice looked down at her white jeans and boat-necked stripy blue t-shirt. And she had been so pleased with her Chanel look!

Devi placed a soft hand on Alice's arm. "I'm so happy you invited us, I've been looking forward to seeing you again. Both Christian and I have." Devi glanced at Christian, who was talking to another man. Devi tapped his shoulder. "Your sister is here, Christian."

Alice's stomach back-flipped as she looked at her brother. He didn't turn round. He was laughing at something the man had said. Had he only come because Devi had made him?

"That's a potential new client," whispered Devi. She stepped aside as a little girl, pizza clamped to her mouth, brushed her leg as she passed.

Flaming ovens at the back of the restaurant raised the temperature and Alice felt beads of perspiration on her forehead. The chatter intensified and she could not hear Christian's voice. Moments later, pinned against the wall by the throng, she lost sight of him too. She was beginning to regret suggesting a meet-up at Emilio's. Christian seemed more interested in Devi and his new client. Alice flopped against the wall. Her legs felt weak, as if they were about to buckle beneath her.

"Are you alright, Alice?" said Joe in her ear. "You're looking a little pale there."

"I'm fine." Alice's throat dried as she spoke.

Joe took a doughball from a proffered dish and listened to the waitress naming the selection of accompanying dips. Alice wiped moisture from her forehead with one of Joe's handkerchiefs.

"Alice." Christian appeared beside her. "It's good to see you."

The siblings looked at each other. Christian's eyes were bright, his skin more tanned than a few days before, his body more relaxed.

"I've missed you," he said.

Alice put a hand on his shoulder. Christian wrapped his arms around her and hugged her. Alice pulled away and squeezed Christian's arm.

"Thank you for coming," she said.

"And miss out on free pizza? No way!"

Antonia handed them each a large slice of pizza. "Sit down," she said. "There are plenty of empty seats." She guided them to a little two-seater table, just inside the swing doors to the kitchen. "Here. You can talk and eat."

"So, you look chilled, Christian, you must have had a good week."

"No work! You see it does wonders for your state of mind. Though I wish I could say the same for you, Ally. You looked stressed."

"No clients, no money, two dead bodies and three suspects. Work is killing me!"

"Or lack of it." Christian wiped his hands on a paper napkin. "What's happened to your clients?"

"Oh, the Renton Hall job is still on. But I haven't been paid." Alice pointed to the photo on the wall above them. "That was another job. But it's finished now and I don't have anything else lined up. Anyway, enough of me moaning. Tell me what you've been up to."

"I've been helping Devi organise the launch of her next collection." Christian pushed up his shirt sleeves and leaned towards Alice. "It was my idea to hold it at a restaurant I know in Soho."

"So Devi told me."

"It's the perfect location and luckily it was available."

Christian outlined his plans for the event. Catering by a local Indian restaurant, a sitar player, the models he'd booked. His face lit up, his hands flew around.

"It all sounds amazing. You're getting really involved with Devi's business. What will she do when you go back to work next week?"

Christian leaned back into his seat. "I may not be going back." He tapped the table as if to reinforce the point. "Devi loves the work I'm doing for her and she thinks I should do it full time. Events planning, that is. I could even set up my own event management company."

"That's great." The words sounded enthusiastic even if the voice did not. "If that's what you want to do. But don't you need some experience?"

"Not really. Look, it's just launches and weddings. And honestly, if you've organised any sort of big party before, then you know what to do."

"I suppose. Of course you know all about the finance side of things through your accountancy work."

"I do. I've seen how these companies operate. All too often, they run into trouble when they don't pay enough attention to cashflow." Christian pointed at Alice. "Like you. If I were you, I'd send Eleanor Carberry a polite but firm email asking her to pay up within the next five working days."

"Well, I'm delighted that you've discovered something you enjoy doing so much. That's very exciting."

"I've flirted with the idea of setting up my own company before, but Devi's really encouraged me to go for it. She's *so* inspiring." Christian threw his arms across the table.

"She certainly is. She—"

A waiter tripped and knocked his tray against Alice's shoulder.

"Scusi," he said, putting a hand on Alice's arm. "I'm sorry, so busy today."

Christian said, "Look, why don't we go somewhere quieter, then we can have a proper chat."

The Bull's lounge was practically empty, so Alice plumped for the sofa by the window. She moved the Sunday papers so Devi could sit next to her. Joe and Christian ordered coffees at the bar.

"I don't remember when I ate so much pizza," said Devi. "But it was really good."

"It's the real thing," said Alice. "Emilio told me that he sources most of his ingredients from Italy." Alice's stomach rumbled. She had been so wrapped up with Christian that she had forgotten to actually eat. "I've been hearing all about your launch, Devi. It sounds as if it's all going well."

Joe and Christian joined them.

"Christian is doing such a great job of organising everything. I don't know what I'd have done without him. He's going to be a big success in the events planning business."

"That's a big change from accountancy, Christian," said Joe.

"It's time to do something that really interests me." Christian patted his quiff. "Up to now, I've just been an observer, while other people enjoy the success of their own businesses."

A waiter laid a pot of coffee and a plate of shortbread biscuits on the table.

"Still, setting up on your own is a dicey business, as you will know," said Joe.

"Christian has the perfect experience." Devi took a cup from Joe. "He's seen how other companies run into difficulties. He's already highlighted areas where I've been going wrong."

Alice took a biscuit. "I wouldn't have thought you had any problems, Devi, what with your high profile. You must be making a good profit."

"I am at the moment. But acting is an unpredictable business and I don't know if I can sustain my profile in the future. Christian's made me think about what would happen to my business if I was not in the spotlight so often."

"You just need to think of all the possible scenarios," said Christian. "You don't want to run into any nasty surprises down the line. Like Cheryl Horton."

Alice spluttered as a piece of shortbread caught in her throat. "How did you know that Cheryl's swimwear business is in trouble?"

"She told me. Eleanor had said to her that I was some hotshot accountant and she wanted some advice. We met up and Cheryl told me the whole sorry tale."

"Well, don't stop there, Christian. Tell us what happened."

Christian put a hand across his chest. "I can't Alice, that would be breaking a confidence."

"Are you saying you're advising her professionally now?"

"No, no, it was just a friendly chat."

"So, spill Christian."

Christian looked out of the window. "Alright. I can tell you that her latest swimwear range is not selling like she hoped. And that means she has cashflow problems; serious ones. She borrowed money to tide her over, but she had existing debts and needed to borrow even more. She was running out of options, so she took desperate measures."

"You see what I mean, Alice," said Devi. "It can happen to anyone."

Alice supposed it could. But Cheryl did not have Devi's name and global profile, nor her bank of resources. "Hey wait a minute. Desperate measures?" said Alice. "Like what?"

"Alice." Christian pulled what Alice supposed to be his corporate client face. "I can't tell you any more."

"It doesn't sound good, though," said Joe. He looked at Alice and raised his eyebrows.

"It's not, and it's further complicated by the loan she had from Nick's company."

"Nick's company lent Cheryl money?" Devi and Alice said together. They looked at each other.

"I can't give you the details, but seeing as you've all ganged up on me ... Cheryl asked Nick for a loan. Instead of giving her money from his personal account, he took it out of the ad agency's account and asked her to pay it back quickly. She'd borrowed money from him in the past and – she was a bit vague on this – I got the impression she hadn't paid it all back." Christian placed his hands on his knees. "Anyway, when Cheryl didn't pay, Nick got aggressive and threatened to sue her."

Devi opened her mouth, but threw the loose end of her scarf over her shoulder first, as if giving herself time to find the right words. "Nick would never have been aggressive towards a woman." She pouted. "That's so out of character. And threatening to sue a family member over money? I just don't believe it."

Christian held up both hands. "You wanted to know what Cheryl said and that's what she said. Though I'm not surprised Nick wanted the money repaid quickly –

after all he shouldn't have used company funds in the first place."

"And to make sure his business partner didn't find out?" said Alice.

"Perhaps. But I think he was just being gentlemanly and trying to save Cheryl's blushes. She was obviously desperate if she had to resort to borrowing money from Nick."

Alice looked at the others, then took a third biscuit. Nobody was counting!

"So, Cheryl borrows money from her brother-in-law, he asks for it back and then he dies," said Joe.

"And if that doesn't give Cheryl the perfect motive for murder," said Alice, "I don't know what does."

Christian slapped a hand against his thigh. "You see, that's why I didn't want to tell you. I knew you'd twist it into something it wasn't. And now you've turned her into a murderer."

"Christian, I—"

"It's typical." Christian stood up. "Alice, I just can't have an adult conversation with you."

And with that, Christian stormed out the door.

Chapter 18

A PAIR OF WHITE tails bobbed along Renton Hall's driveway. The rabbits ducked under a hedge when Alice stepped out of the Defender, re-emerging near the house. Concentrating on following their journey, Alice missed the step into the house and tripped against the front door.

Inside, she went in search of Eleanor. There was nobody downstairs and the conservatory door was bolted, but she heard voices as she climbed the staircase. She went into the bedroom suite at the back of the house, where Gina was studying her phone. Wearing a black trouser suit and a bowed white silk shirt, she took off her glasses and put them in her jacket pocket.

"Ah, you are just in time, Alice. Come and see the colour I've chosen for the bedroom."

Gina took Alice's arm and guided her from what would be the lounge section of the suite, through an archway and into the bedroom itself. A decorator was rolling paint onto the walls.

"What do you think? 'Robin' – it is a good colour, no?"

Alice peered at the striking yellow on the wall. "I think you mean canary."

Gina shrugged. "*Qualsiasi cosa tu dica.* Whatever you say."

"But I do like it."

"There will be a big double bed here." Gina turned to the side wall and spread her arms. "So, you can see out of this bay window and onto the lake. It will be a beautiful room. The curtains and bedcovers will be peacock blue; I get that bird right, no?" Gina smiled.

"It sounds lovely."

A mobile buzzed from the other side of the archway and Gina ran for it. Alice retrieved her bags and headed to the attic, where she found Eleanor shutting the cabinet that housed the guns and pill boxes. Eleanor stepped away from the cabinet and her cheeks flushed a little as she fiddled with a button on her shirt. Wilson had made himself comfortable on the chaise longue.

"Good Morning Alice. I wasn't expecting you so early. I was just checking something."

Alice would liked to have asked what she was checking, but questioning a boss who owed her money was not the smartest of moves. "I'm going to get started on that wardrobe in the corner today."

"In there are the contents of the cabinet of curiosities that Wilfred kept downstairs in the library; bits and pieces he'd collected over the years. It was still there when I was a child. There was a sheep's skull I remember. It used to terrify me and I wouldn't go into the library after dark." Eleanor smiled.

"It sounds fascinating." Alice put her bag on the desk. "By the way, I was walking through the wood the other day and I discovered a pet cemetery."

"Oh, that's the Trevelyans'. It's been there for years; Nick and I used to play in it. Bill shooed us away one day, but we went back when he wasn't around."

"I found a statue of a dog there, a greyhound."

"Oh, that ghastly thing. Bill had it made to commemorate a special greyhound he'd owned. Not that I remember seeing a dog like that around."

A shout from outside took Eleanor to the window. "That's the man about the drains."

"I thought the wood was part of your property, but you say it belongs to Bill Trevelyan?"

"That's right. Funny, Nick asked me the same question recently. He wanted to put in an outdoor swimming pool and he was looking at a spot past Jeremy's snug. As you saw from the plans, the boundary lies along the Renton Hall edge of the wood. But Bill has always let us wander through the woods whenever we wanted."

"Talking of the plans, how did you get on with Gina?" said Alice. "Did she agree to hang them in the entrance hall?"

Eleanor swung an arm across her body. "I'm trying to think of a way to hang them without asking her."

"Ah. Perhaps that's best." Alice watched her foot slide across the floor. "On something else, Eleanor … my fee. Would you mind—"

"Of course, I'll sort it out this morning." Eleanor rubbed her hands. "Well, I must go and see about the drains. I brought you a fan from home, by the way. It gets hot up here and you can't open the windows anymore. If you need another one, let me know."

Alice looked after Eleanor as she disappeared down the stairs, Wilson trailing behind her. Then she crept over to the mahogany cabinet. Keeping her hands locked together behind her back – she was not going to make that mistake again – Alice peered through the glass. The service revolver was not there – it would be locked up in the evidence room at the police station. But otherwise, everything was back to normal. The shattered shelf had been replaced and the collection was back in its original place. So what had Eleanor Carberry been doing?

Alice had not heard from Nathan Salisbury since their meeting, which she assumed meant he could not confirm her as a suspect. Though she knew that he would be dogged in his search for evidence. Alice could only hope that she had not said or done anything else incriminating.

She opened the wardrobe door. It was jammed with objects wrapped in bubble wrap or newspaper. She sighed and turned on the radio. She had put on a thin t-shirt and shorts, but she was already feeling flushed. Eleanor's fan was small, but new and effective. It was also loud.

Alice reached for the objects at the top of the wardrobe and unwrapped newspaper from the first. Inside was a handful of shells – round ones, long ones, shells with holes – and accompanying them was a little piece of card with '*Galway Bay 1925*' written in black ink. Good man! That made the inventory a whole lot easier.

There followed a globe of the world in 1893, a test tube with a tiny lizard immersed in clear liquid, a South African calla lily flattened and dried. Then a pocket watch on a gold chain, a child's footprint preserved in plaster of Paris, a framed piece of card covered in foreign coins. And a sheep's skull.

Alice unwrapped a glass bottle labelled 'Poison', in faded red capital letters. She held it in her palm, newspaper between bottle and flesh. Was the bottle empty or full when Wilfred bought it? Alice tipped up the glass, revealing a label on the base: '*On holiday with Edith, Broadstairs*

1937. Dearie me! Surely it wasn't holidaying with his wife that had prompted Wilfred to buy poison!

Alice was laughing, so when she heard a male voice say, "And now for today's other joke," she assumed it was the radio presenter. Simon Newgate was almost at her shoulder before she realised he was there.

"An empty bottle of poison? Remind me never to accept tea at your house." He grinned and wandered over to the plan chest. Simon put a finger through a hole where a sheep had once gazed over a verdant meadow. "Wilfred's stuff, I assume? I seem to remember they had a few of his eccentric pieces in the library at one point."

"There was a cabinet of curiosities there, apparently."

"I don't remember a whole cabinet."

Alice turned off the radio. "I'm sure you haven't come all the way up here to look at a sheep's skull."

"Not a skull, a sculpture. Nick's father had a statue of Achilles in the dining room, which I always liked. Nick didn't want it and he was going to give it to me. It's up here apparently."

Alice put down the poison bottle. "Oh, I've seen that." She clicked her fingers and pointed at the desk. "It's in that box."

Simon lifted out a small bronze statue of the Greek god, sword in one hand, shield in the other. "Fabulous isn't it?"

"It is. And I'm sure I recognise it from somewhere."

"Hyde Park. This is a miniature of the one in the park."

"Of course. The enormous statue by Hyde Park corner." Alice nodded at the figure. "That's some six pack he has!"

"And I bet he looked like that in real life too."

"The Greek gods were just myths."

"They were. But if Achilles *had* been a real person, he probably would have had a six pack like this!"

Simon roared with laughter, and Alice joined him.

"Anyway, enough of that." Simon replaced the statue and tucked the box under his arm. "I need to find my bureau."

"Is it that bureau over there?"

"No, I think it may be in the conservatory. The police asked Eleanor to clear the hayloft. After they removed Jeremy, they wanted to examine the floor or something. So, they've piled the furniture into the house. Poor Eleanor has now got Gina on her back about that too!"

Alice pictured the steps up to the hayloft and her discovery of Jeremy Evans' body. She shook her head to remove the image.

"The bureau's for my study at home. I bagged it before Jeremy could take it to auction."

"So, you had a rummage through the furniture too?"

"The Carberry's have always bought quality furniture. Quality everything." Simon tailed off and looked at the box. "Luckily, I was free to pop over last Tuesday to have a look."

When Simon headed downstairs to hunt for the bureau, Alice picked up Eleanor's fan, holding it in front of her face. It was effective, but it only gave a small dose of relief. She would have to ask her boss for a bigger fan.

Alice opened the top drawer of the plan chest, where Eleanor had left the plans for Renton Hall. She took the first sheet out, laid it flat on the desk and traced around the boundary line with her finger. The estate was rectangular in shape, with the house at the bottom and the bulk of the land extending to the north and west. In the bottom left-hand corner of the sheet was the official Land

Registry stamp, with '*1972*' written by hand. That must have been the year that Eleanor's father bought extra land from his neighbour.

Which meant that these was not the original plans. There had to be another sheet showing the estate when Wilfred Carberry purchased it. Alice turned over the paper and found a sticker on the back, marked 'Dingle & Son'.

Alice looked up the company and recognised the shop-front that appeared on her screen. Dingle & Son was a property and land consultant with an office on the edge of town and they might know where to find the original plans. She would drop into their office and find out. She was getting behind with the inventory, but she needed to confirm ownership of the pet cemetery and stone dog. And besides, she was boiling.

Alice turned off the fan and made her way downstairs, where she found Simon Newgate talking to Eleanor in the conservatory. Alice smiled, thinking of their Achilles six-pack conversation. Simon was more relaxed today than he had been when Alice had met him in his office. And funnier too.

Inside the Defender, Alice gathered her hair, twisted it into a bun and secured it with a scrunchie. She was just putting the key in the ignition when in her rear-view mirror she caught sight of Simon and another man carrying a bureau out of the house.

It was only then that she registered the significance of Simon's visit to pick out the piece of furniture. He had been in the hayloft on Tuesday the week before. The day Jeremy Evans was murdered.

Chapter 19

An old farmhouse had served as Dingle & Son's office for fifty years, since the business had expanded and moved from Great Wheaton's high street. The receptionist scurried away to find an available consultant, while Alice waited by the open door. Sooner than she expected, a man wearing a green tweed waistcoat marched across the reception area, stiff arms swinging in time with his steps.

"You've found the right spot by the door there. Jolly hot today." He clasped Alice's hand and gave it a firm shake. "Roger Bland. How can I help you?"

"I'm working on the Renton Hall refurbishment and we want to hang a copy of the estate plans. The ones we have are dated 1972, which is when George Carberry bought an additional block of land, but we're after the originals. Specifically, the location plan from when Wilfred Carberry bought the estate."

"And those won't be the originals either. The estate would have changed many times over the years before that," said Roger.

"I'm sure it has, but we're only interested in the period that the Carberrys have owned the property."

Roger nodded and pushed red framed glasses up his nose. "In that case, walk this way."

That wouldn't be easy, she thought, and stifled a laugh. She followed him over the stone-flagged floor and they entered a large square room with rows of filing cabinets and chests.

"This is our records room. We had it specially built fifteen years ago, as we were running out of space in the main office."

"Is there a record of every property transaction you've handled?"

Roger ran a hand through thick salt and pepper hair. "Pretty much. The original Mr Dingle was fastidious about keeping records. He had big ledgers recording every sale; they're with the Dingle family now. But he also kept copies of the contracts he drafted and spares of all the plans he worked on. Now, let's see where Renton Hall's papers are."

Roger consulted a laptop on a small desk in the corner, while Alice wandered along the numbered cabinets. Dingle & Son was the oldest land consultants in the town, and its filing system held a social history of the area's families and businesses. It witnessed their successes and failures as they bought and sold property.

"Ah, here we are," said Roger. "Renton Hall was bought by Mr Wilfred Carberry in May 1913, from a Mr Joshua Littledown. And the records are in cabinet five."

He retrieved a large brown envelope from the filing cabinet. "We'll take it into to my office."

Roger tipped out the contents of the envelope onto a table: a scroll of white paper tied with a red ribbon, together with a large sheet folded several times.

"This is the one we need." Roger stretched out the sheet, flattening it with his palm. "Here we go."

Alice put both hands on the table and leaned over the sheet, tracing her finger along the black line marking Renton Hall's boundary. "This isn't it," she said. "This is just another copy of the plans we already have."

"Are you sure about that?"

"Absolutely." Alice turned over the sheet and pressed a finger against the '*1972*' written in black ink.

"So it is." Roger rubbed his chin. "This needs further investigation." He pressed keys on his own laptop. "Yes, we do have the original plans, it looks like they've been filed in the wrong place. They're in the other room."

Roger appeared a few minutes later and unrolled another sheet. Alice traced around the boundary. With the exception of the new land acquired in the nineteen seventies, the boundary of 1913 was exactly the same as on the 1972 plans. That would mean that the wood and pet cemetery had always belonged to Bill Trevelyan.

"It seems our record keeping is not as fastidious as the original Mr Dingle's." Roger grimaced. "But I'm glad we could help in the end."

As Alice drove home, a rumble from her stomach reminded her that she had not had lunch, so she turned into the high street. She would have the pizza she had missed the day before.

Emilio sat Alice at the same table she and Christian had occupied at the opening. She thought of her brother and how their meeting had been going so well. He was relaxed and happy, he seemed pleased to see her. And then he'd snapped. Alice put a hand to her head. She was too hungry now to work out Christian. She took in each of the Gambi family photographs on the walls. There were enough pictures to be interesting, but not so many as to be overwhelming. Sensitively framed, sensibly spaced and hung at the right height. Good job!

An enormous pizza was placed in front of her and the waiter handed her a cutter. Alice ran the implement across the circle of lusciousness, the round blade slicing through the dough like a hot knife through panna cotta. She closed her eyes and bit into the crisp base, savouring the sweet tomatoes, creamy mozzarella and fragrant basil. Perfecto!

"Do you mind if I join you?"

Alice opened her eyes to find Harry Horton sitting opposite. "This is the only available seat. I didn't expect it to be so busy."

"Of course. I suppose people are buzzing from yesterday's opening and the word has got around."

Harry glanced at the menu. "We would have come too, but Cheryl had a last minute meeting and couldn't get away." He jabbed the menu at the wall. "I believe you were responsible for curating the photos. They look good."

"Emilio selected the ones he wanted and I had them framed and hung. I'm pleased with how they turned out."

Harry ordered. "So, how are you getting on with the inventory at Renton Hall?"

"It's slower work than I anticipated. I didn't realise there were so many small bits and pieces tucked away."

"The Carberrys have always been collectors. I don't remember them ever getting rid of anything."

"They have some wonderful things. It's a pity they can't all be displayed in the hotel."

Harry's pizza arrived and he refused the cutter. "Eleanor tells me the interior decorator is a dragon. Won't let her hang the things she wants."

Alice smiled. "We will have to work on Gina!"

Harry picked up a slice of pizza, hesitated, and put it back down on the plate.

"Alice," he said. "I just want to say, on behalf of Eleanor and myself, that we don't believe for a minute that you had anything to do with Nick's death."

Dough caught in Alice's throat and she coughed into her napkin. She took a gulp of water.

"DI Salisbury called on Eleanor at home and I happened to be there at the time. He said they'd found your fingerprints on the murder weapon. The service revolver. And that he was treating you as a suspect."

It was the second time in two days that Alice's stomach had lurched and her face burned while sitting on the same seat.

"Eleanor explained to him that you were doing an inventory and that, of course, you had to pick up the ... piece. All above board."

"And what did DI Salisbury say?"

Harry picked up the same pizza slice again. "He said that he could see why you had touched it. But that he had to thoroughly examine every clue nevertheless." Harry blushed. "That goes without saying, but you as a murder suspect ..."

So, Nathan really was treating her as an actual suspect. "Did Nathan say what other lines he was pursuing?"

"He was going to interview Simon Newgate after he left us. About time if you ask me, he's the obvious suspect." Harry finally bit into his pizza.

"What makes you think that?"

"Simon was angry with Nick over his relationship with Devi, because it cost the agency her account. A pretty lucrative one too. But also," – Harry looked behind him and leant towards Alice – "Cheryl told me that Nick had lent someone money from the company. Which he shouldn't have done. And then they couldn't pay the money back."

Cheryl Horton was a cool customer. She had fed her husband her own story and passed it off as someone else's.

"And I guess Simon found out," said Alice. "Did he confront Nick about it?"

"Nick and Simon did have a furious row about money, apparently. And that was the day before Nick died. Nick was upset about it and he confided in Eleanor. He told her his concerns about Simon and his worries about their future partnership. So, together with the Jamaican invoices, you see why we're so sure it was Simon who killed Nick."

Alice did see.

"I just wish that Nick had told me. I could have helped him." Harry's voice wavered, but he swallowed hard. "I would have done anything for Nick, anything at all. He's family after all."

When Alice thought of family, she thought of Christian. Their father had disappeared years ago, their mother was living her own life with a new husband. There was Aunt Tracey of course. Alice had fond memories of her aunt, but contact had decreased over the years and they rarely saw each other anymore. That just left her brother. Alice could not imagine her life without him. At the end of the day, Christian was really all the family she had. And she would do anything for him. Even welcome his relationship with Devi.

Alice looked at the top of Harry's head as he finished his lunch. She believed that he would have done anything for his cousin, Nick. He could not possibly have killed him. But the same could not be said about Harry's wife.

Chapter 20

SUDDENLY, THE RECEPTION AREA had furniture. Sofas, easy chairs, side tables, a coffee table. Gina spread her arms and turned a circle on the new carpet.

"So, here is the hotel reception. It is good, no?"

Alice took in the pale blue sofa with its brilliant peacock and pink flower print, the easy chair with feather-patterned cushions.

"It's bright and fun. And I love the colours."

"We still need curtains and some little finishing touches, but it is welcoming, you think?"

"Oh, absolutely, and I like how you've tucked the reception desk in the corner. You don't see it at first, so you feel as though you're walking into someone's house."

Eleanor smiled. "Thank you, Alice, that was the effect we were looking for."

Alice caught a large oil painting on the wall between two windows. A profusion of daisies – white, purple, lilac – bulged from a white ceramic vase. It was simple, but stunning.

"This painting …" Alice said to Gina. "Did it come from your dealer in Paris?"

"That one, no. I bought it for another client, but in the end, I didn't like it in the space. But here, it works very well, so now everyone is happy."

Gina's mobile buzzed and she went into the dining room to take the call.

"Eleanor." Alice stroked the top of the sofa. "I wanted to ask whether you'd had a chance to—"

"I'm making payments later, I'll do yours then. It's just getting the time to do all these admin tasks." Eleanor looked to the floor, so she missed Wilson jump onto one of the sofas. Alice shot forward, arm outstretched, but not far enough to touch the dog.

"Get down, Wilson!" yelled Eleanor.

The dog gave his mistress a fierce stare, then sauntered to the edge of the sofa, hovered for a moment and hopped down. Eleanor rubbed a hand across a peacock breast, now sporting a couple of terrier pawprints. "Oh dear, it needs cleaning already."

"Actually Eleanor, I was going to ask you about the Renton Hall plans. You said you wanted to hang them in here?"

"That was my idea. I thought they could go in that spot just inside the front door."

"I wondered if you had the original plans, that is the ones from 1913 when your grandfather bought the estate. The location plan you showed me was the updated version, it just added the additional land your father bought."

"But it shows the estate as it is now, which is the point I think." Eleanor bent down and grabbed Wilson's collar. She dragged the dog with her and disappeared, presumably to find some cleaning products.

Now that Alice had seen the first furnished room of the new hotel, she had a better idea of how the whole building would look. Gina's descriptions were one thing, but they did not show the depth of colours or the feel of textiles. Alice genuinely liked the reception area and she was excited to see how the other spaces would work out.

She was determined to keep up her end of the bargain and recommend artworks for the hotel. She cleared a space on the trestle table at the far end of the attic to collect her pieces together. She retrieved the Margaret Thomas wild flowers painting, Simon Newgate's gift. Although Eleanor had marked it down for auction, Alice loved the piece and it would work perfectly in the hotel. She needed to convince both Eleanor and Gina to use it and she was not giving up without a fight.

Alice added the plans for Renton Hall and the South African calla lily. Plus a watercolour of a heron painted by Eleanor's grandfather, and a photograph of Wilfred with his new bride, Edith, on their wedding day, which Alice had found in the plan chest. She wanted to add one of the sculptures from Jeremy's snug, but she would collect that later.

Alice lay on the beanbag in *Daisy*'s saloon sucking on an apple and ginger drop. Laptop on her knees, she hovered her fingers over the keyboard. She had no other jobs lined up and her fledgling business would nosedive if she did not land another client soon. She scanned through the emails. Apart from one polite 'No thank you', the rest were from companies looking for business from *her*.

Roddy lumbered down the companionway with a canvas tucked under one arm.

"Am I intruding? I can leave if you're working."

"Come on in, this is a work-free zone." Alice could not thaw the ice in her voice.

Roddy propped the canvas against the coffee table and plopped down onto the sofa. "Oh dear, business still not going well?"

"Not really, no. I don't have any future work booked and the clients I have now won't pay me."

"Now there's a familiar story. People and their money are practically impossible to separate. And, in my humble opinion, the more money people have, the less keen they are to part with it."

Alice put her laptop on the coffee table. "That's certainly true of Eleanor. Livvie told me that she hasn't paid her bill for the party food Livvie did for her. And as for Emilio Gambi, the devil. When I had lunch at his restaurant today, he waived the bill, saying he'd take it off my invoice!"

Roddy threw back his head and roared with laughter. "Paying you in pizza, I love it."

Alice wasn't laughing. "The trouble is, I'm fast running out of money and soon I won't be able to pay my own bills."

"Joe will tide you over for a short time won't he? And living in his apartment must be cheaper for you."

"I give Joe something towards bills and food. But I still have *Daisy*'s costs too, so if anything it's more expensive. And I'm not asking Joe to help finance my business, he'll think I'm hopeless."

"Dear girl, if anyone understands your situation it's Joe. He's been through all the same things when he set up his own company." Roddy put down his canvas and took a sweet from the jar on the coffee table. "Besides your money worries, is life with Joe improving?"

"Maybe." Alice hesitated. "I think I need some time to get used to it. It still feels odd to be at the same address as somebody else."

"It does mean that you can't just do what you want when you want. I think it's good for us to consider somebody else's needs before our own. You miss it when you don't have to."

Roddy avoided her eye. After the sudden death of his fiancé when he was in his thirties, Roddy had had a string of failed relationships as he struggled to cope without his soulmate. Eventually, deciding life would be more straightforward if he lived alone, he bought the creaking barge next door to *Daisy* and resumed his painting. And life *was* more straightforward. But sometimes it was lonelier too.

"How is your work going, Roddy? Is the exhibition coming along alright?"

"Yes, it is. And I've brought something to show you." Roddy picked up the canvas and held it upright on the kitchen counter. "What do you think?"

The languid river scene, a small farmhouse amongst yellow and green fields looked familiar, but Alice could not place it.

"I love the painting, the colours and forms. It's definitely the best landscape you've done recently. Where did you paint it?"

"From the end of my barge. It's our own dear river."

Now Alice began to see the resemblance. "But it looks different, very different. It's the style, no the colours." Alice put a finger on her lip. "Okay, tell me, what have you done?"

"I've painted it somewhat in the style of Cezanne. I hope that doesn't sound pretentious. See, the simplified shapes, the square for the farmhouse and the rectangular fields. But also I've copied his blocks of strong colour."

"And all those short brushstrokes," said Alice. "Horizontal for the river and vertical for the trees ..., of course, I can see it now. The River Nare through the eyes of Cezanne, what an interesting idea. But what made you think of it?"

"Boredom. I'd finished a few paintings and they were starting to look a bit samey, so I felt like doing something different. I've always loved Cezanne's landscapes and I experimented with his techniques in this picture. I was worried it wouldn't work, so I'm relieved you like it."

Alice clapped her hands. "You could do more paintings like that, I mean in the style of other artists. That would be a hoot. How about a vase of cowslips in the style of Van Gogh's sunflowers?"

"Or the Nare in the mist à la Turner."

Alice threw her arms wide. "Or algae on the river in the style of Monet's dreamy water lilies." They both roared with laughter. She hadn't laughed so much in a while, and it felt good.

When they settled down, Roddy said, "Dearie me, we got quite carried away there. Anyway, that's me sorted. Let's see if we can sort you out."

Roddy took a sweet out of the jar and wandered over to Alice's incident board. "Wow, that's got some bite!"

"I think they overdid the ginger, but it's alright once you get used to it."

"Still three suspects, I see?"

Alice peeled herself out of the beanbag and stood beside Roddy.

"Actually, we can eliminate Harry Horton." Alice unpinned Harry's picture and scrunched it into a ball. "I met him today at Emilio's and he's devastated by Nick's death. He said he would have done anything for Nick and I believe him. Besides, I was talking to Harry at the time it happened, so he couldn't have done it."

"Dear girl, I hope you're not getting sucked in by fake tears and a pseudo sob story. As Sherlock Holmes said, even if something looks impossible, you can't eliminate it because people pretend to be idiots!"

Alice slapped her hand on her thigh. "He did not say that."

"Probably not. But what I'm sure Sherlock Holmes would say, is that you can't dismiss a story until you have proved that it can't be true. Ergo, I wouldn't be so quick to dismiss Mr Horton."

Alice frowned at the ball in her hand. She looked back at Roddy. Then she straightened Harry's picture and re-pinned it to the board.

"Cheryl Horton's money problems," said Alice. "She's obviously desperate to keep her company afloat. Borrowing money and not paying it back isn't a good look in a murder scenario."

"I agree she's a strong suspect. And Simon Newgate?"

"He's my prime suspect. He was at Renton Hall the morning I discovered Jeremy Evans."

"Again, agreed."

Alice rubbed finger and thumb together. "How are you getting on with your hunt for blondie?"

"Disastrously! Do you know how many men with blond hair live in Great Wheaton? Hundreds! I fear I've set myself an impossible task."

"Well, I think we need to find him. I feel sure he must be around here somewhere."

Roddy tapped Jeremy Evans picture. "I don't understand why poor Jeremy was also killed."

Alice planted the tips of her fingers under her chin. "Everybody seems to have liked him. It's a mystery."

"Almost as mysterious as the fabled dog."

"My thoughts exactly. I did find a dog, a grey stone thing, in the pet cemetery in the wood dividing Renton Hall from its neighbour. I assumed the cemetery belonged to the Carberrys at first, but it appears that it belongs to Bill Trevelyan next door."

"And?"

"And I was thinking there could have been an argument over land, a dispute about the boundary. But the plans on that side of Renton Hall's estate haven't changed in over a century. I'm beginning to wonder whether Sarah Evans has led me down a blind alley on that one."

"So, what do we conclude from this little chat?"

"I am in need of one suspect, one brother and a whole lot of clients."

Chapter 21

Alice pulled drawers open in Joe's kitchen, looking for a tin opener. She was going to surprise Joe with a rare home-cooked dinner and she had dug out what was described as an 'easy' spaghetti with tuna sauce recipe. But controlling multiple pans on a hot stove, working out instructions and using the right ingredients was not her forte.

A pungent smell of garlic filled the kitchen and Alice pushed vegetables around a frying pan with a wooden spoon. She searched for spaghetti and, spotting it jutting out from behind the toaster, grabbed one end. As she did so, a siren blared above her and she looked up to see the red light from the fire alarm flashing on the ceiling.

She leaped over and was stretching up to turn off the alarm when Joe rushed into the room.

"Hey! What happened?" He threw his keys onto the table and pushed a button on the box.

It fell silent and Alice heaved a sigh. "I was just cooking dinner."

"Is that what you call it?" Joe pointed to a trail of spaghetti on the floor.

"Oh no." Alice held up the near-empty plastic wrapper. "I didn't realise it was open."

Joe bolted past and took the frying pan off the burner, plunging it into the sink. He switched off both gas rings and turned on the extractor. Alice peered into the pan and saw squares of blackened onions.

"Rats! I only turned my back for a second. I'm sorry Joe, I wanted to cook dinner for you." Alice bent over the sink, trying to hide her burning face as she scraped off little bits of burnt onion with the spoon.

Joe gently rubbed the back of her neck. "Hey, no worries. Leave that." He eased the pan handle from her hand. "We'll go to The Bull for supper."

An extra glass of wine encouraged Alice to unburden her client worries to Joe over dinner, so the next morning he took her to work with him. His friend had agreed to photograph a local businesswoman at home, but then found he had double-booked himself and asked Joe to cover for him. Joe did not know either the woman or the house, so he figured he could do with another pair of hands. The shoot would just take the morning and Alice was only too happy for an opportunity to make up for her cooking disaster.

Barbara Roseland's son invited Joe to set up wherever he felt appropriate; his mother would be down shortly. Joe and Alice wandered into the dining room, a minimalist affair with a long black table, grey carpet and bare walls. Next door, a pale pink and green living room with plump cushions and woolly throws, was more inviting, but it too had bare walls.

"So, what do you think?" said the sultry-voiced chief executive.

"Gosh." Alice took in the traffic light red of Barbara's fitted dress. "It looks amazing."

"Thank you, but I meant the backdrop." She shook hands with them both. "Where would you like to set up, Joe?"

Alice sucked in her cheeks and looked at the floor.

Barbara smiled. "I'm glad you like the dress. I was just trying it on. I'm taking my husband out for an anniversary dinner tonight and I wanted to make a special effort."

Joe picked up his camera case. "As the pictures are for the financial pages, I think the dining room is best. I'll set up in there."

"Good, that's what I thought too. I'll put on a suit, won't be long."

Joe had everything under control, so Alice sat down to watch. The shoot did not take long. Which was a pity, because Alice had not seen Joe at work before and she was enjoying the experience. Joe gave Barbara directions, which instead of sounding like instructions, came over as friendly advice. Alice noticed how quickly Barbara relaxed and did as Joe asked, responding to his praise with little giggles. Alice also noticed that Joe did nothing to discourage her!

Joe finished shooting and began discussing the images with Barbara, so Alice volunteered to make coffee. She strolled through the hallway and into a large breakfast room. On the fridge, photos were held in place by a red lobster magnet, its legs wobbling as Alice opened the door. There were no pictures on any of the walls. Alice mentioned it to Barbara when she returned.

"Well that's a bone of contention between Tony and me. We have completely different taste and, frankly, can't agree on how to decorate the house. That's why this room has Tony's preferred utility look. But I got to do the living room and that's another style altogether." Barbara added milk to her coffee. "We have a collection of paintings which we both enjoy, but we can't agree on where they should go."

Alice looked at Joe, but he was removing a lens from his camera. "I could help you, if you like." Was it inappropriate to pitch her services on Joe's job? "I'm a curator and I could advise you and your husband on where to hang your art."

Joe smiled his approval.

"That could be the answer," said Barbara. "We have some good pieces, but they're languishing upstairs in the spare bedroom. It's such a shame."

"Well, think about it." Alice pulled a card from her bag. "Just give me a call and I can come over and chat to you and your husband."

Barbara took the card and put it on the table. "Actually, we could talk now. I had blocked out the whole morning for the shoot, but Joe's been so efficient." Barbara grinned at Joe. "I've got some spare time. Give me a minute to get changed." And before Alice could respond, Barbara was jogging through the door.

Joe zipped up his camera bag. "Well I see you didn't waste any time. Looks like you've got a new client."

"You don't mind do you?"

"It wasn't my job to begin with, so we've both got something out of Finn's bad diary management." Joe took the car keys from his pocket. "I need to sort out these pictures, so I'll take your Defender. Call me when you're finished and I'll pick you up."

Barbara, now on her third outfit, saw Joe out of the front door with a giggly smile.

The house was newly built, one of only two on the site of an old riverside warehouse to the south of Great Wheaton. In the style of a Georgian country house, the rooms were large and square, with high ceilings and sash windows. But there was solar-powered heating and a runoff water supply.

"It was the eco features that attracted me to the house. I'm phasing in a series of environmentally friendly initiatives at my company. I felt I ought to practice what I preach, if I'm going to get the staff on board."

The spare bedroom was indeed spare. There was no furniture or boxes of stuff. Just a series of artworks, protected with bubble wrap and propped up against all four walls.

"We've built up the collection over the twenty years we've been married. We just bought pieces we liked, so there's no theme or order."

"I'm glad you said that. I've worked with people who buy paintings for investment purposes and while I appreciate that art is a commodity, it's good to think that people really like the artworks they buy."

Barbara nodded. "And I would love to get this lot on the walls. Somehow." She shut the door as if closing away the rift with her husband. "Alice, can I show you something? I've bought a painting for Tony that I'm going to give to him later. I'd love your opinion."

In her bedroom, Barbara eased an artwork out of a drawer in the wardrobe and handed it to Alice. Rows of bright blue rowing boats packed tightly together, with lines of rope tethering them to a point beyond the area of view. The work had a thick white mount and a thin black frame.

"We were on holiday in Essaouria last month and Tony loved the harbour. So I bought him this in a local gallery." Barbara crossed her arms.

"Simple but effective," said Alice. "And that blue! It's like a royal blue, but richer and highlighted by that white sunlight ... It's just gorgeous."

"Oh, that's a relief. I was about to wrap it up last night when I had second thoughts." Barbara took the painting and tossing some clothes out of the way, she laid it on the bed.

Alice peered at a swimsuit and matching sarong. "I recognise those. They're from Cheryl Horton's beachwear collection."

"They are! So you buy her things too?"

"They're out of my price range, sadly. But I saw a picture of these in her office last week."

Barbara sat on the bed. "So, you know Cheryl? I met her at a businesswomen's lunch a couple of years ago and I've run into her a few times since. I love her designs. How long have you known her?"

"Only a couple of weeks, I met her through Eleanor Carberry. I'm working on the Renton Hall refurbishment."

"That place is going to be fabulous when it's finished. I dropped Cheryl off there one time and got to look inside. And what a wonderful decking area out the back by the lake. They're going to have some great weddings and parties out there."

Alice moved the sarong and sat down. "It's a lovely project. I'm really enjoying the job."

"But it's a whole hotel and a huge project, for you. Look, if you don't have time to hang my paintings at the moment, it can wait. The works have been wrapped up for months, a few weeks won't make any difference."

Alice protested and Barbara tried to insist. In the end, they agreed that Alice would find a few hours that week to view the collection and the house. Then she would work up some ideas and let Barbara know when she was ready to discuss them.

"And please, take all the time you need. There really is no rush. Although, I would like to get them up before Christmas if that's possible."

"It's six months away, so that shouldn't be a problem."

Barbara took Alice downstairs, where they compared diaries and made a date.

"It was terrible about Nick Carberry," said Barbara. "I met him once at a drinks party in London." Barbara sat on a stool at the kitchen counter. "The police have been pretty tight-lipped, I've not heard of any arrests. Do they even have a suspect?"

Alice had almost forgotten that she was Nathan Salisbury's number one suspect.

"Er, not that I know of. Though I did hear that Cheryl might be a suspect." Alice noted Barbara's raised eyebrow. "I mean, of course, everyone close to Nick has to be a suspect, before they can be eliminated."

Was that too leading? Alice may have nudged Barbara towards a negative view of Cheryl. Oh well, too late now.

"I suppose. Though now you've mentioned Cheryl, she comes over as all sweetness and light, but she can be manipulative. I have two business acquaintances that Cheryl, very skilfully I may say, played off against each other. Not only that, but she made sure that she came out on top." Barbara folded her shirt sleeves to her elbow. "We all have our faults and I'm not making any judgements. It won't stop me socialising with Cheryl, but I'd be reluctant to work with her."

"I heard she had money problems too. Do you think there's any truth to that?"

Barbara looked at the clock on the wall. "Probably. In fact, her financial woes are well known on the business-women's network. It seems that Cheryl and money are quickly parted. And that's not helped by the off-beat decisions she makes. She asked me my advice on something once, then completely ignored it. Not that I'm suggesting I'm some corporate genius. But when Cheryl said that other people had already advised the same course of action as me, I thought she might take notice."

Alice considered whether to ask her next question. But she decided that when you are a murder suspect, no question should be off-limits.

"So, given what you know about Cheryl, do you think it likely that, if she got herself into a really difficult financial situation, she could kill her way out of it?"

Barbara hesitated. "Cheryl is often in messy financial situations. But if she found herself in a much worse situation than normal, would that would drive her to murder? I really wouldn't like to say."

Chapter 22

THERE WAS A POLICE car parked outside Renton Hall when Alice arrived. Delighted at having secured a new job and much-needed income from Barbara Roseland, Alice ignored it and skipped into the house. She calculated that once she had deducted her outgoings, she would have a cushion of cash to take her into the autumn. But when she saw Nathan Salisbury sitting on Gina's new sofa in the entrance lobby, Alice stiffened. Nathan could be here for any number of reasons; but one of them could be to arrest her for murder.

The detective stood up and with two easy strides he was by her side. He led her up to the attic.

"I wanted to have a quiet chat with you and I thought this would be the best place."

Nathan beckoned Alice to the chaise longue and sat next to her. Alice had the feeling that this little chat was not going to be much fun.

"After you gave me your account of how you had come to handle the service revolver, that is the murder weapon, I made some enquiries. I did tell you that I would have to verify your story." Nathan turned his shoulders so that he was facing Alice. He probably thought it was more open and engaging than speaking to her side-on, but it only served to make him look bigger and more serious. "So, I've spoken to Eleanor Carberry and Gina Salvini, who were both in the house at the time when you say you picked up the revolver."

Alice's stomach knotted.

"Although they were in the house at the time they were not, of course, here in the attic. They didn't see what happened and that doesn't help you. So, what I want you to do" – Nathan put an arm along the back of the seat – "is to run through your movements again, so I can see exactly what you did."

"You mean like a re-enactment?"

Nathan smiled. "Yes." He stood up. "Let's get started. Tell me what you were doing just before you got to the cupboard. Better still, walk me through it."

Alice acted out the episode, incorporating every single detail she could remember. Nathan watched and listened. He nodded at times, but otherwise there was no emotion on his chiselled face.

"And then I decided to log the contents of this cupboard. I don't know anything about guns, but they looked old, antique even, and I assumed some of them were collectors' items. And that they would be valuable. In any event, my role here is to catalogue everything."

Alice walked across the boards towards the cabinet. She put a clammy hand to her head. "I opened the door so I could see the pieces more clearly. I needed a full description for the inventory. Actually, I should have picked them all up and done a proper investigation; I'm supposed to note down the exact condition of all the items."

"Can you open the cabinet door for me please, like you did before?"

Alice's mouth dropped open. "But then my fingerprints would be on the key."

"Your fingerprints are already over the cabinet and all of the pieces inside. However, if it makes you happier, I'll record the rest of our meeting on my phone." Nathan set his phone to video and propped it up on the back of the chaise longue.

Alice opened the door and was hit with a musty aroma. The first time around the smell had excited her. She felt as if she was the first person in years to open up the cabinet, like opening Tutankhamun's tomb. But now it just smelt like rotting mushrooms. Alice glanced over her shoulder and Nathan gave an encouraging nod. She stretched her hand into the cabinet.

There was a gap on the shelf where the service revolver had been. Improvising, Alice picked up a similar weapon on the shelf below. This one was smaller and not so heavy. As it nestled in her hand, Alice was struck by the gun's ugliness. It was hard to see why people prized such items. The more ornate pieces, with silver filigree, polished wooden grips and healthy price tags, was understandable. But this ordinary handgun had been designed for a specific purpose, and not an artistic one.

"I'm not sure how it happened, but the next thing I knew I'd knocked the shelf and it fell down." Alice knelt on the ground. "There was glass all over the place and some of the objects fell out too. So I picked them up and put them back in the cabinet."

Re-enactment complete, Nathan switched off the camera and popped his phone in his jacket pocket. "Thank you for that Alice. I know it's not easy to re-live these situations, but it helps me to understand the scenario. You were doing a job that involved handling the guns in the cabinet. I believe you."

Alice did not realise that she had been holding her breath until a shot of air escaped through her parted lips. Somehow, she could feel a 'but' coming.

"But, my problem remains the same." Nathan perched on the corner of Wilfred's desk. "I have two dead bodies, one murder weapon with your fingerprints on it and no other suspects."

"Yes, I can see how that would be a problem." Spots of rain tinkled against the big round window. Heavy clouds hung low over the house. Alice felt as if a cloud of steel was hanging over her head.

"However, I have what I hope is a solution. You and I can work together. It's a bit unorthodox, I know, but you did such a great job of solving the Jason Marley case. I mean you got to the culprit long before we did. And this time, you're right here at Renton Hall where the murders took place." Nathan spread his hands. "So, what do you think?"

Alice had no idea what to think. On the one hand, she was flattered that Nathan had asked for her help. And she was delighted that he had finally acknowledged that it was her solo efforts that had identified Jason Marley's killer. On the other hand, she was still a suspect herself. And with her own face on the police incident room's wall, pointing the finger at somebody else would be a bit, well … awkward. But going back to the first hand, Alice did not think she should say no to Nathan. So, she didn't.

"Excellent. I think our arrangement will work well." Nathan punched a fist lightly into the palm of his hand.

"Now, I've got to spend my evening wading through a stack of files that DI Riley's unearthed. A missing person's cold case he's been working on in his spare time." Nathan grinned. "He should get a proper hobby!"

Alice watched Nathan stride across the attic and disappear down the stairs. Would working with Nathan really work? Alice did not mind sharing some information with him, but she could not shake off the feeling that he might be looking for her to slip up. Bringing your main, your only suspect, into the net was just the sort of well-thought-out tactic that Nathan would employ. It was understandable, but should Alice willingly stray so close to DI Nathan Salisbury's net?

Nick Carberry's face peered out from Alice's incident board. Alice put both hands behind her head and stared right back. Two knocks on the side window signalled that her friend was about to appear.

"Come on down, Livvie Manners, and bring those chocolate brownies with you."

Livvie put a cake box on the kitchen counter. "I'm out of brownies, in fact I practically sold out of all my cakes today; these are all that's left."

Alice lifted the lid. Half a slice of ginger cake, a flapjack missing one corner and a cupcake with purple icing. "That's it?"

"'Fraid so. Though as my till has been ringing all day, I'm one happy lady."

Alice took the flapjack. Not her favourite, but it was the biggest of the items on offer. Livvie crouched down in front of the incident board. "So, how's your investigation going? I don't see any coloured string linking pictures together."

Alice held out a hand to catch falling oats. "You've just summed up my problem. I have some victims and suspects, but nothing to tie them together."

"What about him?" Livvie stabbed a finger at the dog picture. "He looks evil."

Alice ripped the illustration off the board, crunched it up and tossed it on the sideboard. "That stupid thing?" She felt heat rise to her cheeks. "I've been taken for a ride on that one."

Livvie lifted a box of sweets from the arm of the sofa. "Hello! What have we got here? Coconut barfi, jalebi … yeah, I know those. But oh my god, look at the others. Those green things – they must be pistachio. And is that gold leaf on the pink ones?"

"I think so. They're Indian. Devi gave them to me, so I expect they're at the luxury end of the market."

"Can I try one?"

"Go for it. By the way, she said those green ones are her favourite. Pass one over, will you?" Alice bit into earthy pistachio marzipan and a sweet, creamy pistachio filling. "I like it. But it's a bit heavy on pistachio. What did you go for?"

"The pink one. It's coconut, but nutty too, cashew perhaps. Utterly delicious." Livvie hovered a finger and thumb over another candy. "You're going to have to up your game on the sweet front from now on." She nodded at Alice's sweet jar on the coffee table. "And these all the way from Mumbai, too."

"Devi bought them from an Indian deli in West London. Though I suppose they came from India originally."

"Wherever. They're ace. How's your bro, by the way? Have you heard anything from him lately?"

Christian had replied to Alice's message, thank goodness, she had not been sure that he would. He had said that he would check in with her later. Alice had read many different interpretations into those few words. She had toyed with the idea of sending a response, even drafting a couple of versions, but she couldn't decide the most appropriate. And she didn't want to make the situation any worse, so she left it. Christian would contact her again soon.

"I'm not sure where Christian is. He's not being very communicative at the moment."

"He's probably busy with Devi's launch."

Alice smiled at her friend. "Thank you for your pragmatic, and probably completely right, answer."

"Good, I'm glad you're not over-stressing about it. So, now that's sorted, let's crack the Renton Hall murders. My money's on Cheryl. Money and love, the two biggest motives."

"I thought that too, but Simon Newgate is not in the clear. And he was on the premises the day Jeremy was killed."

"Just because you didn't see Cheryl at the party doesn't mean she wasn't there. And she was there. You said she was changing when you arrived, but she could have been hiding in the wood, whacked Nick and then run back to the house pretending she'd just found him. Or maybe she sent someone else to do the job for her."

"All true, but it still doesn't give us a clear answer."

Livvie checked her watch. "Jeez, I need to shoot, Steve will be waiting for his pint."

"Don't tell me you and Steve are actually spending some quality time together?"

"We had a big talk and decided that we can't carry on working all hours and never seeing each other. We agreed to have a date night once a month and tonight we're going to The Bull for a quiet drink." Livvie picked up a coconut barfi and left.

Alice's eyes fell on the scrunched picture of the dog on the sideboard. As with Harry's, she picked it up and smoothed out the creases. The dog's stony eyes glared back at her. Sarah Evans was adamant that the dog was the cause of both deaths, and until Alice was absolutely, positively sure that Sarah was mistaken, she had to keep an open mind.

Chapter 23

Eleanor waved at Alice before vanishing into the kitchen, Wilson following behind. Alice raced after her. But the door to the garden was open and Alice stalled. Pursuing her client and Renton Hall's owner into the grounds was a bit over the top. Obviously, the key to staying well-off was to avoid paying your bills.

Decorators were stripping off wallpaper in the room next to the kitchen. Previously used as the Carberry's informal dining room, it would now serve as a breakfast room for hotel guests and double up as a private dining room for hire. Gina had kept the original fireplace, now being painted black. She patted the decorator's shoulder as she talked to somebody else on her mobile.

When the call ended, Gina said, "So, Alice, an informal room for breakfast and at the same time, a formal dining room for special occasions. They make my job difficult, no?"

Had Eleanor paid Gina upfront for the paint the men were using? Or for the curtain track they were replacing and the new curtains that would be arriving soon? Gina's Parisian art dealer would certainly have demanded a deposit to secure the pieces he was buying for her. Thinking of which made Alice ask: "Gina, has Eleanor spoken to you about the Hall's plans? She wants them hung in the entrance?"

"She hasn't, no."

Coward! "Eleanor was very keen on the idea, I'm surprised she hasn't mentioned it."

"We've already discussed my design for that space and I won't renegotiate at this stage. Tsk, am I not busy enough already?" Gina's phone went and it was soon clamped to her ear again.

Alice walked through the conservatory and onto the decking, over the bridge and up the path to Jeremy's snug. The police tape had been removed, but the building felt dark and forbidding. It almost looked as if it was in pain. Alice hurried passed and into the heart of the wood.

She reached the pet cemetery and made straight for the stone greyhound. Crouching down on one knee she inspected the dog thoroughly. She ran her hand over the sculpture from ears to tail, but there was nothing unusual about the weather-beaten ornament. She got up and circled the graveyard. Finding nothing further to detain her, she carried on to Bill Trevelyan's house.

Barleyland's front door was wide open, but when Alice peered inside, the hall was empty.

"Hello," she called, leaning in from the threshold. She heard a male voice from the back of the house and was just about to reply when she recognised it as belonging to radio presenter JC Brown. The Trevalyans were not going to hear her over him, so Alice thumped on the door and stepped into the house. Getting no response, she walked across the hallway and was at the kitchen door before Elsa Trevelyan looked up from her newspaper.

"Good heavens dear, you did give me a fright," said Elsa, pressing a hand against her chest. "How did you get in, by the way?"

"The front door was open. I did call out, but you probably couldn't hear me over the radio."

"Oh, that would have been Bill, he went out to look at the sweet peas. Anyway, now you're here, would you like a cup of tea?" Not waiting for a reply, Elsa emptied tea leaves from a chipped teapot into a plastic box on the drainer and spooned in fresh ones.

"Em, we haven't actually met. I'm Alice. I'm working for Eleanor Carberry at Renton Hall."

Elsa smiled. "I know dear, Nick Carberry told me all about you at his party. He pointed you out." She lifted a kettle from the Aga and poured water in the teapot. "It must be exciting for you, being at the Hall while all that fancy work is going on. I expect I won't recognise the place when it's finished."

A cat dashed into the kitchen. Elsa poured milk into a saucer beside the back door and the animal bolted over, slurping up the liquid as quickly as it was replenished.

"That wretched cat got in again," said a man from the hallway. "It shot past me before I could—" He stopped. "And who are you?"

"This is Alice. She's working with Eleanor at the Hall."

Alice recognised Bill Trevelyan from the party, but he did not appear to remember her. He limped into the kitchen, leaning heavily on a walking stick.

"What are you doing feeding that thing? It'll never leave now."

Elsa put the teapot on a large wooden table, along with three cracked mugs from a Welsh dresser. Bill waved his stick at the cat, which ignored him.

"Sit yourself down and we'll have a nice cup of tea." Elsa pulled out a chair and manoeuvered Alice onto it.

Bill propped his stick against the sink and clutched the edge of the unit with both hands. "You're the art lady Eleanor's got in."

"That's right. I'm sorting through the attic at the moment and I've already found some of Wilfred's pieces that I'm hoping we can hang in the hotel."

"Hmph! I wouldn't want some stranger rummaging through my things after I've gone." Bill folded his arms and fixed Alice with a hard stare. "I bet old Wilfred is turning in his grave."

Alice stirred imaginary sugar in her tea. "Eleanor wants a record of all their possessions, so they can work out what to do with them before the house is filled with paying guests." She knew she sounded pompous, but she didn't care.

Elsa put a hand on Alice's arm. "Don't take any notice of him dear, of course they have to sort through Wilfred's things. Eleanor is only being practical, as always."

Alice sipped her tea and fought to disguise a sudden cough. It tasted like antifreeze.

"Is it strong enough dear? I never know with visitors."

Alice nodded, wiping away a tear. She gobbled the chocolate biscuit Elsa offered, hoping that her taste buds would forgive her. "It will be different for you too, won't it? Having a hotel next door instead of a family home."

"It'll be a big change for us and there's been no consideration given to it," said Bill.

"It'll not have any real effect on us," said Elsa. "The guests are not staying here after all. And Eleanor will run the hotel, so we'll still see her regularly. We miss Mary of course, she was a lovely lady. Though it was right that she moved back with her sister, she was lonely at the Hall by herself after George passed away. And as for Nick …" Elsa put both hands over her eyes for a moment. "Well …"

"He's gone and that's the end of it," said Bill. Alice caught his grimace as he shifted his weight from one foot to the other. "There's a new phase now at the Hall and I suppose we'll just have to get on with it."

"Of course, there's the wood dividing the two properties, so it's not as if we'll see any of the guests," said Elsa.

"But there's the path through the wood," said Alice. "I followed it myself this morning."

"We'll block it off." Bill took a shaky step and grabbed hold of a chair. He leaned towards Alice, dark eyes glaring. "I won't have strangers tramping over my land."

Alice shrank into her chair.

"We'll put up a gate at our end of the path and that'll stop people coming through," said Elsa. "And Eleanor said there'll be signs up at the Hall, telling people this area is private property."

"But what about Jeremy's snug?"

"The police have closed it and it'll stay closed," said Bill. "The same goes for that animals' cemetery. I own the whole wood and it's about time people respected that."

Had Bill been watching Alice when she had discovered the pet cemetery? Nevertheless, Alice had come to find answers and she intended to get some. She took a deep breath and put her mug on the table. "So that dog is yours? The stone sculpture in the cemetery?"

Elsa picked up the teapot. "Would you like a refill, dear?" Alice shook her head. "The Carberrys will always be welcome on our property. I'm sure that Eleanor's children will still want to visit the pet cemetery; we'll be happy for them to carry on doing so. And as for the hotel guests, well there's plenty of land on the Carberry's estate for them to roam around."

"I heard that Nick Carberry had been thinking about putting in an outdoor swimming pool. It would probably be just the other side of the wood from your house. I wonder whether Eleanor will pursue that idea?"

"Not if she's got any sense," said Bill. "Kids jumping in the water screaming their heads off. We'll get no peace around here. Now, I've got things to do." He retrieved his walking stick and stumbled out the back door.

"He's got grumpy in his old age." Elsa smiled. "I have a meeting at the church hall shortly, so I'll see you out."

The women walked along the gravel driveway. There was no sign of Bill, though the sweet peas looked in good shape.

"It's been lovely meeting you," said Alice. "And thank you for the biscuits. And the tea."

"I'm glad you came. I was going to chat to you at the party, but I didn't get a chance. Dear Nick, what a horrible shock it's been."

"It was so sudden. And what happened exactly, is still a mystery. Do you have any idea who might have killed him?"

Elsa stopped and turned to Alice. "Do you?"

"I have some suspects in mind, but I'm not sure about any of them."

Elsa put a hand on Alice's shoulder. "I wouldn't worry dear," she said. "These things always sort themselves out in the end."

Back in the attic, Alice ran through her inventory. She covered her eyes with her hands. The task was far more time-consuming than she had envisaged. Worse, she now realised that she had under-quoted; she would lose money on her first freelance job. She snatched up her phone and sent a firm email to Eleanor, asking for her fee to be paid by the end of the day.

Alice needed to get through the rest of the work as quickly as possible. As she was standing beside an old trunk, she would deal with that next. It was full of papers and photographs, jumbled up together. She emptied armfuls into the wheelie suitcase she had brought with her, zipped it up and headed for *Daisy*. She would work through the material at home, while she looked for other clients who did pay their bills.

Chapter 24

ALICE CLEARED A SPACE in *Daisy*'s saloon and tipped the contents of her wheelie bag onto the floor. Rummaging through the pile, she picked out some notebooks and piled them onto the coffee table to look at later. That left a heap of loose papers, invoices, letters and photographs. Alice grouped them together in manageable sections.

Thinking the invoices would be the least informative, Alice started with those. There were bills for repairs to a chicken coop and the respray of a Daimler Conquest. A bill for the hire of a morning suit and top hat for Bertie Hampton's wedding, had moved Wilfred to write 'charlatan' in big letters across the chit. Whether that referred to the hire shop or the groom, was unclear. The bills were a fascinating insight into Wilfred Carberry's iron grip on the household finances, but, as Alice had expected, they were not much help. She took a couple of pear drops from the sweet jar and flopped onto the beanbag with a pile of letters.

The letters were all written in Wilfred's hand, mostly in black ink. One was a complaint about a boiler service. Written in an authoritative manner, the letter resulted in a reduction of fifteen percent on the bill. An IOU from the local grocer for eggs caught Alice's eye. If those were from Wilfred's chickens originally intended for the family's use, they had provided an entrepreneurial opportunity. Another letter was to someone called Ned, thanking him for his hospitality during a recent visit. It took a second reading of the 'Ned' letter for Alice to realise that either Wilfred had not sent the letter or, perhaps more likely, he had laboriously written a copy to keep himself. Thank goodness for photocopiers!

The letters and invoices exposed another side to Wilfred Carberry, but they did not push Alice's investigation any further forward. The stack of photographs was no more useful.

Alice stretched and went up on deck. The river was as still as a landscape painting. She leant an elbow on the barge's side and looked upriver. Over in Farrell's field, Patches was grazing contentedly, watched by a pair of blackbirds perched on the gate. Alice whistled, and the pony looked up and whinnied.

Back below, Alice opened the first of Wilfred's notebooks. The pages contained columns of numbers, so at first it looked like an accounts book. Except there were sketches too. In one section, headed '*Chicken Coop*', Wilfred had drawn designs for a new home for his birds. Underneath each drawing was a description of the structure and a list of the materials required to build it, together with an estimated cost. Wilfred had come up with three different ideas, but in the end he had decided to repair the one he already had. Clearly it had been thanks to Wilfred's frugality that the farm at Renton Hall had survived and thrived.

The next book was a personal diary, each entry headed with the day and date. The book began on 21 June 1970, with a moan about the weather. It had rained, ruining Wilfred's plan to spend the day painting beside the river. Not wanting to stay inside all day, he had done some gardening and got soaking wet. He dried off then watched horse racing on the television. Mary had served lamb cutlets for dinner – very good – and he had enjoyed a brandy afterwards.

Alice flicked through the book, every line filled with Wilfred's neat writing, recording some observation almost every day. She picked up another diary, this time for 1972. On the back page, her attention was caught by some rare capital letters: "*HE AGREED.*" She read on. "*Agreement to be finalised, but he's broadly happy with my draft. All in all, a good day's work.*"

Alice backtracked and discovered that the agreement was between Wilfred and Bill Trevelyan. Wilfred noted that the two men had met on 7 August to discuss '*the issue*'. Wilfred did not elaborate further, simply recording that the conversation had gone well. Bill had been receptive to his proposal. But Alice could not see the proposal.

She flicked further back, but the pages did not reveal the details. Perhaps he had jotted them down later, in which case they might be in another book. Which Alice did not have. So she got in the Defender and drove back to Renton Hall to find it.

Alice stepped over a cable running from a manhole in the driveway into the hallway, disappearing through a hole in the wall. Decorators, electricians, a man to install satellite television and two men carrying a king-sized bed – the Hall was buzzing. In the library, bookshelves were being fixed to the wall. The space above the fireplace was still empty – Gina's dealer must be struggling to find a suitable piece.

In the conservatory, Devi was talking to Gina, who had both hands on her hips and a glare on her face. Devi beckoned Alice over.

"Ah Alice, I hope you can help us. Gina and I are discussing which fabric to re-cover the seats in here. Eleanor wants a traditional conservatory, so we'll keep the tiled floor and there'll be lots of big plants, but she wants people to be comfortable. She is bringing in big sofas and easy chairs. We all agree on a jungle-type print, but I think it should include some colour."

She handed Alice a swatch of fabric. Amongst the large ferns on the print were pink elephants and yellow flowers.

"But Eleanor said *traditional*." Gina shot her arms in the air. "Animals on seating are not traditional."

"Perhaps not, but without another colour this room will be green and more green."

"And that is the point of a conservatory, no?"

"I've seen colourful flowers in even classical glass rooms, so I can't see your objection to the blooms on this print."

"But elephants! No. There will be no elephants here." Gina's phone rang, but she ignored it.

"Alice, what do you think?" said Devi.

The print looked innocuous enough, but this was one argument Alice was not going to get involved in.

"This is such a beautiful space and with that fabulous view of the lake, I'm sure the conservatory will be lovely whichever fabric you choose."

As her phone buzzed again Gina backed away, muttering as she pressed Answer. "Tsk, how many clients do I have to deal with at once?"

More than me! Not for the first time, Alice wished her own phone rang as often as Gina's. She took Devi's arm and led her away.

"The woman just won't listen," said Devi. "Eleanor wants this print and she asked me to speak to Gina. She hoped that if both of us asked her, we could make her agree. I find it weird that Gina doesn't do what her clients ask her to do."

"Gina's very experienced and she has a formidable reputation, which she protects by rejecting clients' suggestions that she knows won't work. I can see that and I'm sure there are plenty of other interior decorators who would do the same." Alice smiled. "Though I do like your elephants."

"Well, I'll tell Eleanor that I tried. I can't do any more than that." Devi flattened against the wall as a man with a roll of carpet on his shoulder struggled passed. "I need to see that carpet laid. Eleanor can't be here today and she wants me to report back."

In the attic, Alice lifted up the trunk lid. She sat on her haunches and picked out the notebooks. One of them had to be Wilfred Carberry's missing diary. In the end, there were twenty-seven notebooks with the same fawn covers, the word '*notes*' written in the middle. Finding the continuation of the 7 August 1972 entry would mean going through every book.

Alice picked up snippets of Wilfred's jottings as she thumbed through the books. One day he was annoyed that a delivery of cow feed was late. Later on, he was pleased that his son had scored a century in his end of school year cricket match. And delighted that his stag watercolour, painted near his sister-in-law's home, had perfectly caught the animal's majesty. Some of the pages should be framed and hung alongside the Renton Hall plans. The hotel guests would find them entertaining.

A floorboard creaked behind her and Alice looked up. Christian! She fell to one side, placing a hand on the floor to prevent herself toppling. Christian eased across the space between them and offering her his hand, helped her to her feet.

"I don't remember the last time I had that effect on a woman. It's a pity you're my sister!" Christian smiled, revealing newly whitened teeth and bright eyes.

"What are you doing here?" Alice clasped her hands together. "I mean it's good to see you."

"Devi told me you were up here." Christian dug hands deep in his trouser pockets. "Look, I don't like us falling out, Ally. So whatever I said or did to upset you … I'm sorry."

"Me too. I mean, I'm sorry for my part. And thank you for, well … just thanks." Relief, like a heatwave in December, gushed through Alice's body. After sleepless nights agonizing over whether Christian would come back, here he was. And Alice was not going to let him go again. "So, what have you been up to?"

"Big decision." Christian sat on the desk chair. "I'm going to set up my own events planning company. I mean I know I've said that before, but I've spent the past few days thinking about it properly, to make sure it's what I really want. And, well, I've almost started my own business three times already, so it was about time I just got on and did it. So, I have and I've started the process. I've told my boss and handed in my notice."

"That's great news." Alice beamed at her brother. "And you've already got your first job – Devi's launch party."

"Yes. It was good of Devi to give me the project. And it's definitely given me a kickstart."

Alice leant against a wooden post. "Does that mean you'll be based in London now?"

"Yes, that's where the demand is. There's plenty of people prepared to pay good money for someone else to organise their events. Even better, it'll only be a couple of hours' drive to see you instead of the five hour trip we have now."

Being closer to Christian would be amazing! The physical distance between them had been a major reason for the limited occasions they had seen each other. Ten hours' driving had meant committing a whole weekend to the trip.

"Well, perhaps you can find me some clients, too," said Alice.

"Why, are things not going well for you?"

"They're fine. Renton Hall is a big job and I've got another one lined up afterwards. But," – Alice lowered her voice – "getting money from them is like pulling teeth. Only one of us wants to do it."

"Welcome to the real world!" Christian threw back his head and laughed. "The key is to have lots of clients. If you have more work than you can cope with, then you should be able to get money in regularly."

My thinking exactly! Though it was working out how to reach more people that was the problem. Perhaps advertising would help.

"What's your business called by the way?"

"Alice Haydon Freelancing"

Christian frowned. "You might want to come up with something more catchy."

Alice had wondered that herself. Time for a rethink. Or even a proper razzmatazz launch like Devi's.

"How's the clothing launch party going?"

Christian swirled the chair from side to side. "Really good. It's going to be brilliant, you must come; twentieth September."

"They're well designed clothes, I wouldn't mind buying some myself. When are they available for sale?"

"Devi will give you whatever you want, just ask her. No, I'll ask her."

"I couldn't. Of course I'll pay."

"Don't be silly. Besides, I know you'll wear them and then you can tell people they're Devi's!"

Alice admired her brother's wily tricks – she could learn a lot from him. She could even ask him to be involved in her company. Perhaps a sleeping partner?

"I didn't think this job would involve you crawling around on the floor."

"Actually, Christian, you can help me. I'm looking for the other section of one of Wilfred Carberry's diary entries." Alice put up her hand before Christian could say anything. "Don't ask. I'm hoping it's in one of these, so could you help me look for it please?" She gave Christian a handful of books. "There should be an entry on the first page, saying something about an agreement Wilfred made with his neighbour Bill Trevelyan. I need to know what that agreement was."

If Christian wondered whether his sister was going a little loopy, he showed no sign of it. He opened up the first book. Alice did likewise and they worked their way through them all.

"It's not here, Ally."

Alice agreed. "It's possible the page could have fallen out, these books are over forty years old."

"Or perhaps Wilfred tore it out and put it somewhere else."

The pair got up and Alice piled the books on the desk.

"Hey!" Simon Newgate was standing at the top of the stairs. "I came by to drop something off to Devi and she said you were up here. I thought I'd come and say hello."

"She must be getting tired of directing people to the attic," said Alice.

"I would ask what you're up to, but it feels like there's a long explanation and I've got a train to catch. We should have a drink some time and a proper catch-up. I'll call you at the weekend." And without waiting for a response, Simon disappeared.

"I suppose he's sniffing around Devi's business again now that Nick's gone," said Alice.

"Can you blame him? It's a lucrative account. And I'm only running her events, so I'm not in his way."

Thunder sounded overhead and charcoal clouds coloured the window. Alice stood by the glass.

"No matter what the weather's like, there's always an interesting view from here."

"I suppose water plopping onto a lake does have its charm."

Christian stood beside his sister. Alice felt her brother's warmth beside her. Thank goodness they were talking again. And this time, she would not let them fall out over some silly remark. Christian's relationships were none of Alice's business. Besides, it would be cool to have a Bollywood star in the family.

Lightning flashed across the lake, thunder cracked and Alice flinched away. So she did not register the whizzing sound that passed her ear. But she did hear a loud crack from somewhere behind them, and glass crashing to the ground. She inched around and saw a hole in the window, a spider's web of cracks around it.

"Get down!" Christian put a hand on Alice's head and pushed her to the floor. "Someone shot at us. And they're close by."

Chapter 25

ALICE'S FACE WAS PRESSED to the floorboards, dust collecting in her nose and throat. Christian had thrown himself on top of her, and gallant though this act was, he was preventing her from breathing

"We'll hide behind that sofa thing," said Christian. "Get behind me." He got to his hands and knees, pulling Alice by her sleeve. "Let's go." He crawled to the chaise longue and sat on the floor, his back against the seat. Alice tucked in beside him.

Alice's racing heartbeat echoed through her ears. She put a hand on her chest and took a deep breath. What on earth just happened? Alice stared at the window. It did look as if a bullet had passed through it – somebody really had tried to shoot them.

She tapped Christian's shoulder. "Did you see anyone out there?"

"No. But it's so dark, I can't be sure. I'll check."

"No." Alice tugged his arm. "Let's find a light first."

Christian nodded and the pair looked around. The only light was from a small anglepoise, which did not spread further than the edge of the desk. The switch for the main light was by the door and getting there would involve crawling across the attic floor and exposing themselves to anyone still lurking in the attic. A tall standard lamp was closer. Its flex trailed along the wall, but Alice could not see a plug.

Christian and Alice both reached for their mobiles and switched on their torches. They crawled around the side of the chaise longue and cautiously stood up. Making their way across the attic, they waved their beams underneath the desk and behind cupboards. But there was not the faintest sign of another person.

"Let's go back behind that sofa thing, while we work out what to do next." Christian took Alice's hand and they returned to their safety position.

Alice's instinct was to shut the door at the top of the stairs to stop their attacker coming back. But her legs felt like blobs of clotted cream; she could not rise to her knees let alone to the door.

"Did we just get shot at?"

"Let's not talk about that now."

Good advice! Alice turned her mind to practicalities. "How are we going to get out?"

"I was going to ask you the same thing." Christian gave a wry smile.

"We could stay here until someone comes up and rescues us."

"We could. But let's come up with a more practical suggestion ..."

Alice looked up at the window. "We could just make a run for it. We've checked out the attic, there's nobody here."

"There wasn't when we looked, but whoever was here before could come back."

That seemed unlikely. Take a shot once and run away, but come back for another go?

"I think it's probably clear by now."

Cannonball rain pelted the roof. Water blew through the hole in the window and sprayed across the floor.

"Boo!"

Alice screamed. She clutched Christian's arm with both hands, pushing her face into his shoulder. She felt a tug to her hair and heard a voice, though it was indistinct against the thunder. Alice drew her legs to her chest and burrowed deeper between Christian and the chaise longue. But her brother moved, and she would have dropped to the ground had she not been caught in a firm grip.

"Alice, look at me!"

Alice turned around. Devi was shaking her arm. "Goodness me, what silly game have you two been playing? You look scared half to death. You almost hit the roof when I said boo."

"Simon Newgate shot us," said Alice. "Shot at us."

Devi released Alice's arm. "Are you sure?"

"Look!" Christian pointed at the window.

"Oh my god." Devi reached out a hand towards the glass.

"We should go," said Christian. "Simon, or whoever did this may still be in the house. And we're trapped up here."

Alice nodded and took Devi's hand. Christian peered over his shoulder once and nodded. He made for the stairs, the two women close behind. At the bottom, Alice scanned the area. There were decorators and maintenance workers scurrying around, but she could not see Simon

Newgate. At the front door, she ignored the weeping sky and ran for the Defender.

Inside *Daisy*'s saloon, Alice made coffee.

Devi picked up the box of Indian sweets she had given Alice. "I see you've had a few of these, did you like them?"

"Livvie and I loved them. Beautiful flavours and very different from what we're used to."

"Good. I'm thinking of launching my own sweets range, so you should both come to a tasting session."

The hatch door opened. "Can I come in?" said Roddy. Without waiting for an answer, he clambered down the steps. "I thought I'd come and see if there was another dance session in the offing."

Alice glared at him. He dropped his smile and sat down.

"So how come you're all here?" said Roddy.

"Christian and I were shot at in Renton Hall's attic."

"Dear girl, not again? Your curating life is turning into a one-woman combat zone."

"Again?" said Christian. "This has happened to you before?"

"Long story short, yes. But let's not get into that. We need to figure out what happened to us today."

"That's exactly what you should do." Roddy said. "But first, I'm going to pop home and fetch a necessary aid." He disappeared through the hatch door.

Alice held up her incident board. "I think we can presume that whoever shot us has something to do with the Renton murders. I started with three suspects and whittled that down to two – Simon Newgate and Cheryl Horton. I've got motives but no proof. But I am convinced it was one of these two people who just attacked us."

"Simon must be the prime suspect as he was at the Hall today," said Devi.

"True. But I think we need to go back to the beginning on this." Alice took a notebook from a drawer in the sideboard. "We need to write down everything we know about the murders and the suspects and pin it on that board." She tore out sheets of paper and handed them around, together with felt tip pens.

Roddy returned with a bottle of rum. "Here we go." He poured a measure into Alice and Christian's coffee. "And a non-alcoholic version for Devi that a friend won in a raffle. But don't let that put you off, I'm told it's very good."

Alice did not like rum as a rule, but in warm coffee, the sticky sweet flavour was soothing. She knocked back the rest.

"Now." Alice addressed the group. "Simon Newgate. As Devi says, he was at the Hall today and as I'm assuming that Cheryl wasn't there ..." – she waited for confirmatory head shakes – "we'll take him first."

Alice thought Simon slick and polished, much as she imagined an ad man to be. But he had not said or done anything to make her think he was capable of bumping off his business partner.

"I suspected Simon from the word go." Devi flicked back her hair. "He wanted Nick out of the way, so he could have the whole business to himself."

"I heard that from Harry Horton too," said Christian. "Whose opinion was that Simon wasn't as good a businessman as he thought he was."

"There were the Jamaican invoices that Harry mentioned." Alice rolled a pen between her fingers. "Do you know anything about that?"

"I think that's what Harry meant," said Christian. "There was some financial blip in the company and Simon was responsible."

"People make mistakes," said Roddy. "There might have been a rational explanation for what happened."

"That's true. Harry didn't tell me the details, and as far as I'm aware there was just the one incident."

"But it involved a lot of money and Nick had to cover the cost from his own pocket." Devi jabbed with her pen. "By that time, the agency was no longer working for me, but if I had still been a client, I would have had grave concerns about how the company that handled my business was being run. If Nick hadn't stepped in so quickly, it could have been a disaster."

When Alice had asked her about it, Cheryl had been spare with details about the money she had borrowed from Nick. Perhaps the Jamaican invoices involved nothing more than Nick lending his sister-in-law some cash. He might have taken the money out of the company because it was his quickest access to funds, then paid it back from his personal account. But why was it referred to as the Jamaican invoices?

"What I don't understand," said Christian, "is why Simon wanted to get rid of Nick at all. The London office he fronted brought in most of the agency's clients and it was largely down to Nick's own networking skills."

"And that was the point." Devi shuffled on the sofa to face Christian. "Simon didn't like Nick being out at the front of the business, meeting all the new clients and taking the glory when they signed with the agency."

"Then again, Simon must be a good manager of the back room and you need both those types of people to make a business successful," said Christian. "You know, it's like Wham. Everyone remembers George Michael out the front, but the band wouldn't have worked without Andrew Ridgeley, who did the non-glamorous bits in the background, without any fuss. The combination made them global stars."

Roddy twirled a section of grey beard. Then he poured himself an extra large measure of rum. Alice stared at the blank sheet of paper in front of her, but all she saw was a window. With a bullet-hole in its centre.

Devi's phone rang and she rummaged in her bag. "I need to go, but I hope we've been helpful, Alice. Please contact me if you need any more information on Nick's business."

"I will. And thank you for being so calm and sensible back in the attic."

Once Devi and Christian had gone, Roddy slumped into the sofa and stretched out his legs. "Dearie me, they are a charming but exhausting pair. And I didn't understand a word they said."

"I thought their insights would be helpful, but now I'm more confused than ever."

"I always think that too much information is a dangerous thing. The details cloud the central issue."

"Hmm, you're annoyingly right. As usual. I've been asking people about Simon and Cheryl, but all I'm getting are opinions. Nobody seems to know anything for sure."

Roddy picked a sweet from Devi's Indian box. "It was always thus. By the way, these are delicious. The box is almost empty, which may have something to do with me."

"I'll buy some more when my clients pay me. But first, I've got to find the Renton Hall killer before they get to me again." Alice held up her incident board. "One of these people is the murderer. But which one?"

"Are you sure it is one of those people? It could be someone else altogether. Someone who hasn't made it onto your board."

Alice examined her suspects. If not them, then who? There was Eleanor Carberry. But could Eleanor have killed her own brother? She would not be the first to do so, but Eleanor clearly adored Nick. There had been lots of guests at the Carberrys' on the night of Nick's death. Any one of them could have killed him and Alice had only met a handful.

But Jeremy Evans was different. He had no high-profile business and no glamorous Bollywood girlfriend. He lived a quiet life tending the grounds of Renton Hall and pottering around his own garden with his attentive wife. How could he be a threat to anyone?

With her investigation going nowhere, Alice propped the board back in its place and looked at Roddy.

"I think I'll have to rethink my strategy. And I know exactly where to start."

Chapter 26

When Alice arrived back at Renton Hall, the cable had been removed from the doorway, but now there was drilling coming from the dining room. Alice went into each room noting the people that were there and what they were doing. Having not done so that morning, she did not know whether any of them were the same people. But if there was another attack, she might at least have the comfort of knowing she had seen their face before.

At the top of the stairs, Alice shut the attic door behind her. There was no lock, so she dragged a box of broken crockery in front of the doorway. It would not stop a determined intruder, but they would make a lot of noise when they opened the door. Alice turned on every light. She had brought one of Joe's torches with her and she turned it to full beam.

Alice cleared Wilfred's desk and sat down in the leather chair. She opened the top drawer and looked again for Wilfred Carberry's missing diary. But she had no luck. She tried an adjacent chest of drawers. She had been through it before, but she could have missed a stray notebook amongst the voluminous papers. But no, the diary was not there either. Alice turned to Wilfred's bureau and had just opened the drop-down writing surface when she heard the sound of smashing china. Someone was trying to open the door.

"Alice? Are you in there?" Eleanor nudged the door again.

"Just a minute." Alice moved the box to one side and Eleanor stepped inside.

"What's that doing there?" Eleanor rubbed her calf. "And, good heavens, you've got every light on."

Alice led Eleanor to the window and pointed to the spider's web of cracks with the hole in the middle. "Somebody attempted to shoot me and Christian earlier. Fortunately, they found the glass instead. But as I'm up here by myself, I put the box by the door so I'd know if anybody came in."

"Are you sure that was caused by a gunshot?" Eleanor put a hand to her cheek. "Did you actually see somebody shooting?"

"Thc shot came from behind us. We thought they might have another go, so we ducked down. By the time it was safe to move again, whoever had been here was gone."

"And you've no idea who it was?"

"No. There were lots of people in the house at the time. It could have been anyone."

"I'd better call the police. DI Salisbury will want to see this."

"Don't worry, I'll call him. I need to give him an account of what happened anyway."

Eleanor slipped on the wet floorboards as she turned to leave, clutching the chaise longue to stop herself from falling.

"Oh dear, look at the mess. I'll send someone along to wipe up the water. And board the window."

Alice heard a scratching sound and turned to see Wilson's backside in the air as he shoved his nose behind the bureau. He jumped back and pawed at the ground, growling as he did so.

"There's something behind there he wants, probably a dead rat." Eleanor called the dog, but he ignored her. She reached behind the bureau and pulled out a rawhide chew. "I was looking for that, it's a favourite. I wonder how it got there?" The dog jumped up and Eleanor patted his nose. "You'll get it when we're home."

"Before you go, can I just ask you—"

But Eleanor was already halfway out the door. Wilson turned around and sniffed the air before following his mistress downstairs.

It was only by chance that Alice glanced down, otherwise she would not have seen the notebook poking out from behind the bureau. She stooped down and picked it up. On its fawn front cover was the word 'notes', just like all the others. Could it be ...?

Alice opened it up. It *was* the missing diary. On the first page, Wilfred Carberry had written about his agreement with Bill Trevelyan:

Bill agreed to sell his stone greyhound at the price I suggested. I will draw up a formal agreement and we will both sign it in the presence of Cookie Miller. Bill happy that I keep the agreement at Renton Hall.

So, it was about the dog after all. But the actual agreement was not there. Alice flicked through the notebook, but there was no further mention of it. She looked around the attic. She would have to go through everything again, this time looking for a piece of paper signed by Wilfred and his neighbour Bill. It was going to be a long afternoon.

All the workmen had disappeared by the time Alice descended the stairs. She had Wilfred's notebook tucked in her bag, but she had not found the agreement. She shouted a goodnight to Gina at the far end of the conservatory and left.

She sat in the Defender and checked her bank account. No new deposits. With Eleanor's sloth-like attitude to paying bills, it could be ages before Alice received any money and *Daisy*'s rent was due soon. The owners were understanding people but Alice had always paid her bills on time, and this was one payment she was not going to miss. She sent an email to Emilio Gambi asking him to pay his outstanding invoice immediately.

Her phone buzzed and Alice read Joe's text. His train had been cancelled and he would be late for dinner. Alice had arranged a meeting with DI Nathan Salisbury. She would see him first and pick up a takeaway afterwards.

When Alice called Nathan, he suggested they talk over a drink at The Bull. He found a quiet spot in a corner underneath a shelf of old brass tankards and was thumbing keys on his phone when Alice set down their beers.

"Just had to send that email," he said, putting the phone in his jacket pocket. "I'm all yours. Now, tell me about today's incident."

Alice described the whizzing sound she had heard, followed by the damage to the window and her assumption that she and Christian had narrowly avoided a bullet. She recounted Simon Newgate's visit and the many people who had been milling around Renton Hall at the time.

"But I can't believe Simon had anything to do with it. If it were me, I would want to make a quick getaway before I got caught."

"That's my feeling too," said Nathan. "Though sometimes the perpetrator goes back to see what effect their action has had, whether they had actually hit their target, so that they are prepared if questioned. But Mr Newgate doesn't strike me as being that brazen."

"Me neither." Alice sipped her Peroni. "I'm thinking that the person who came after me today – and I'm sure they were aiming for me – must be the same person who killed Nick Carberry and Jeremy Evans." Alice looked at Nathan's impassive face and noticed his soft eyes, as though for the first time. "Am I allowed to ask who your suspects are?"

"You can ask, and I'm telling you this in confidence. And by the way, yes, I think you were the target of today's incident." Nathan put both hands on the table. "I had Simon Newgate as a suspect, but also Cheryl Horton and her husband. Though I am not so convinced about Harry. Whilst I have my suspicions, there's not enough evidence to make an arrest. The investigation has come to a standstill and I'm looking for something new that will give us a breakthrough."

Alice looked at Nathan. If things had worked out differently, this could be her and her boyfriend having a cosy drink. When Nathan had re-entered her life back in the summer, Alice was agonising over her relationship with Joe, playing with the idea of moving in with him. Nathan was calm and steady; he made no demands on her. She had seriously contemplated finishing with Joe for Nathan. But her decision had worked out for the best. Her relationship with Joe had moved into a new and enjoyable phase. And Nathan had remained a friend. So, as a friend, Alice told Nathan about Sarah Evans' preoccupation with the dog, and Wilfred's reference to an agreement.

"It's certainly an odd arrangement."

"Here, you can see for yourself." Alice handed over Wilfred's notebook. "It's on the first page."

Nathan turned over a few pages and flicked through the rest of the notebook. "The agreement itself is not here. Have you seen it?"

"No. I've looked in the attic, but I haven't found it yet. But even without it, what do you think?"

Nathan closed the book. "It could be two fastidious, old-fashioned men making a genuine transaction and doing it formally because that's the way they did things. But it seems like a lot of trouble to go to over a garden ornament."

"That's what I thought. And the sculpture is very ordinary. These days you could buy something similar in any garden nursery." Alice opened her own notebook. "I did a bit of research on this and dropped into Beecham's Nursery on the Cornbury Road. They were there back in the late sixties, early seventies. They told me they did stock a range of garden sculptures at the time, including a dog. Though it wasn't the same as Wilfred's."

"What about other outlets? There would have been more nurseries around at the time."

"I asked them that. There were others, they said, but the only one they thought might have sold these sculptures is on the way to Cambridge. I could ask them I suppose."

"Leave it, I'll get one of my team to follow it up." Nathan made a note on his phone. "Of course, we're just taking this statue story at face value. There could be something more pertinent beneath the surface."

"You mean something hidden inside?" That had not occurred to Alice, but now that Nathan mentioned it, it seemed an obvious possibility.

"The statue's been outside for years so it can't be anything that would rot or otherwise deteriorate."

"And it has to be something small, about this size." Alice's hands drew a rough nine-by-six-inch rectangle in the air. "Like jewellery. Or they might have stolen some gold bullion ... Or perhaps its the ashes of a murder victim."

"Now you're getting carried away." Nathan laughed. "Though you may be onto something. If a precious object is hidden inside, it would explain the formality of the Carberry and Trevelyan agreement. I'll come over tomorrow and have a look at the area. I can take the statue away for inspection."

The pair agreed to meet outside Jeremy's snug the following morning. They chatted about Alice's freelancing work and Nathan's sponsored charity walk. Finishing their drinks, they wandered into Great Wheaton's high street. Nathan turned left and headed up the hill to his home. Alice turned right and into China Fang to pick up dinner.

Chapter 27

IT SEEMED AS IF Gina Salvini never slept. She was the last person to leave Renton Hall in the evenings and the first to arrive in the morning. So Alice was not surprised to see Gina when she arrived at just after seven the next morning.

"I'm about to make coffee. Would you like an espresso?"

"I would love one." Alice had a quick look into the downstairs rooms. "How's the work going? You looked very busy yesterday."

"I wouldn't be so busy if people did what they were supposed to do, no?" Gina took Alice's arm and steered her into the kitchen. "But I know people are unreliable, so I work it into my schedule. The hotel will open on time."

The kitchen was the only room still in its original state. Eleanor had insisted that there should be one space in the house where she could sit down without workmen flitting around her. Gina had agreed to finish the library first, so that Eleanor could use that room while the kitchen was refitted for commercial use.

"I'm glad you're here early." The coffee machine finished gurgling and Gina handed Alice a cup. "I can show you a painting that arrived yesterday from my dealer. This is the piece for the library. You remember we discussed this before?"

Alice remembered thinking that Gina's brief to her dealer would be almost impossible to fill. She was looking forward to seeing what he had come up with. Gina unwrapped the painting and gave it to Alice.

"It's a good work, no?"

No! About two feet square, a lonely snow-topped mountain, coloured blue, with a necklace of green trees, was overlooked by one thin cloud. The piece was not badly painted, but it was not quality workmanship either. It was not offensive, but it did not say anything. It was just… blah. Still, top marks to the dealer for coming up with a piece at all.

"It's … interesting."

"Good. And I'm sure Eleanor will like it too."

Alice gulped her coffee and walked into the conservatory. The black and white tiles were gleaming. The iron framework around the glass had a new coat of green paint. She opened the door and stepped onto the decking. Early birds sang in the trees, a rabbit hopped beside still waters. Alice ambled over the wooden bridge and into a spray of pale mist hovering above the field.

As she neared Jeremy's snug, Nathan Salisbury came into view. He was accompanied by DS Nick Riley.

"Murky morning." Nathan looked to the sky. "Still, it should clear up soon."

The trio made their way through the wood to the pet cemetery. Already gloomy trapped as it was beneath the trees, with the additional mist the area had an especially eerie air.

Nathan put a hand on the stone dog's head and glared down the animal's back. "So this is it?" he said taking a torch from his pocket, he shone the beam around the sculpture. "Can't see an opening. I thought there might be a join somewhere."

"You could use some more light." Nick Riley shone his own torch around the bottom of the statue. "It's hard to see properly, but if someone had hidden something inside, they could have made an opening underneath."

"Good thinking. I'll tip it up and you have a look." Nathan stood behind the dog and tugged its head. But it did not budge. He put his foot at the base and tried again. "It's not shifting. It must be pinned down."

Nick Riley pulled on a pair of gloves and brushed leaves and moss away from the base. "Ah, here we go."

Nathan and Alice crouched down beside him. Nathan picked at a rusty clip attached to one of the dog's toes. He traced his finger along the metal strip, stopping when it reached the ground. "See if there's another one on the other foot."

Alice and DS Riley looked together. There was.

"Hey," came an angry voice. "Get away!" Bill Trevelyan hobbled towards them. When he saw Alice, he shook his walking stick at her. "Who are these people?"

Nathan pulled his ID badge from his pocket. "I'm DI Nathan Salisbury and I'm leading the investigation into the recent murders at Renton Hall."

"Well they weren't anything to do with me. So you've no need to be on my land."

"And who are you, sir?"

"Trevelyan fom Barleyland. Next door. And what are you doing on my land?"

Nathan folded his ID and put it back in his pocket, zipping it closed. Bill leant on his stick, slapping his other hand against his thigh in the manner of an agitated cat.

"We have reason to believe that this sculpture is relevant to our enquiries. I'm taking it away for forensic examination."

"Forensic examination! For something that had nothing to do with what went on over there?" Bill poked his stick towards Renton Hall. "That's my dog. You need my permission to take it away. And I'm not giving it."

"This sculpture could reveal a vital clue and we need to give it a thorough examination. We'll only have it a few days."

"I'll be on to your superiors. I know the chief inspector. He'll vouch for me."

Nathan strode across to Bill. "This is a murder investigation, Mr Trevelyan. You can contact my boss if you wish. But time is running on and leads are getting cold. I would appreciate your cooperation."

Bill growled. He turned his back on Nathan and limped away.

"Is the neighbour always that friendly?" said Nick Riley.

Nathan smiled and looked around him. "We need some cutters if we're to get this dog off the ground. Do you know where we can find some, Alice?"

"Jeremy kept tools at the back of his snug."

Nathan sent Nick to the snug, and in the meantime he strolled around the cemetery reading the headstones. "Bit depressing having a graveyard on your property."

"That's one way of looking at it. Though I suppose somebody thought the children and perhaps the adults too, would like a proper resting place for their pets. And when you've got money to spend on these things, you can afford your own cemetery."

"Are you sure it's only animals? There aren't any of the family buried here?"

"Not that I know of." Alice wiped the bench and sat down. "I had assumed the family members are buried at St Edmunds." Alice looked at the clip on the stone dog's foot. "What do you make of it, Nathan?"

"I think the fact that such a heavy stone sculpture was pinned to the ground, strengthens your theory that there's something hidden inside. Let's hope that's the case when we see the base."

Steel clanking on steel sounded through the trees. Nick Riley was pushing a wheelbarrow with a selection of tools clattering inside.

Nick picked up a steel bolt cutter. "I think this should do the job. Though I've brought a hammer and a cold chisel as back up."

Nathan snipped at the fastening with the cutters, sending rust flakes into the air. At the second attempt, the clip snapped. He despatched the bolt on the dog's other foot and freed the sculpture from its shackles.

"Right, let's try again." This time, when Nathan tugged the dog's head, the sculpture tipped over. "Riley, we'll lift it onto the bench. On my count …" When Nathan said three, the men picked up the dog and settled it on the seat.

"It's not as heavy as it looks," said Riley.

"It must be hollow." Nathan turned to Alice. "Which is what we thought." He rubbed earth from the sculpture's bottom. "It's too dirty to see anything. We'll get it cleaned up, then we'll be able to see what it's hiding."

They lifted the dog onto the barrow and DS Riley wheeled it off, with instructions to take it to the police van at the front of the house. Alice crouched down beside the pale square on the ground left by the sculpture's removal. She ran a hand over the stubby dead grass.

"Nothing there?" said Nathan.

"No." Alice was about to stand up when she noticed a length of string caught in a tuft of grass on the edge of the patch. She held one end between finger and thumb and followed it through the weeds to the bench. The other end was tied around one of the seat's metal legs.

"I wonder how long this has been here?"

Nathan ran a finger along the string. "It looks like nylon, so it could have been here ages."

"Forty-five years?"

"Conceivably. Why? Do you know what it means?"

"Maybe." Alice combed the grass on the other side of the sculpture's resting place and found more of the same string. She pulled it, but it was buried beneath the soil, a gentle tug insufficient to release it. "I don't want to pull it any harder and risk breaking it."

"I'll get it dug up."

"You might want to do that." Alice rubbed soil from her hands.

Nathan reached for his phone, turned away and spoke a few words. Alice meandered along the edge of the cemetery and into the heart of the wood. She patted the bark of an old oak tree and weaved around a skeletal ash. A couple of conifer trees reminded Alice of Christmas. She wondered whether the ring of stumps she found were trees that had been felled by the Carberrys for the festivities.

There was another clump of conifers further on, these ones were reddish-brown instead of the rich green of their neighbours. Like the ash, they were succumbing or had succumbed to disease. And there were many others. Alice spun around. The trees were close to the Renton Hall side of the wood. She ran back to Nathan.

"I've got it." Alice gasped, catching her breath. "The agreement has to be about an exchange of land between the two men. Wilfred didn't register the change of boundary officially, because he thought his agreement with Bill Trevelyan was good enough."

"And they used a piece of string to do that?"

"Well it was a neighbourly arrangement! I think their agreement was that Bill would sell part of his land to Wilfred. And they marked the new border with string."

"Well they certainly didn't execute a formal sale," said Nathan. "We checked."

"But Wilfred Carberry either owned, or was about to own, more land. Though what he would have done with it, is hard to see."

Nathan looked around the area with its odd little cemetery. "I can't begin to imagine."

"But we do know that his grandson wanted to build a swimming pool for his hotel using land close to the wood. Many of the conifers have died, so I wonder whether Nick planned to clear them away and do something useful with the land."

"And we'll assume that his neighbour didn't like that idea."

Bill had made those grumpy comments about noisy kids jumping into pools. "Probably not."

Nathan collected the cutters and they set off back down the path to Jeremy's snug. "We'll work on the dog and I'll let you know what we find."

When they reached the building, Nathan headed off to help lift the sculpture into the police van. Alice pushed the door, creakier than she remembered and tidied the tools away. What would Eleanor do with the snug once the hotel was open? They would always need somewhere to keep tools, but Jeremy's living area, still welcoming and comfy, would not serve any obvious purpose.

And what of the string boundary? It made sense that the formal agreement between Wilfred and Bill was about something important like land. It seemed likely that Nick Carberry had found out about it. Perhaps he confronted Bill and the ensuing argument might have ended with Bill killing Nick. It sounded plausible enough. But without that agreement it was only guesswork.

Alice's phone buzzed; a text from Emilio Gambi telling her that he had paid her fee for the photographs. Hurrah! Now she could pay *Daisy*'s rent. And she might even treat Joe to dinner. In a restaurant.

Alice's muddy fingers had left smudge marks on the phone's screen, so she went to the sink to wash her hands. She used the rose-scented soap resting on a glass dish and wiped her hands on a fluffy towel. The Evans' had really made this little hovel a home from home – no wonder the Carberry children had such fond memories of the place.

Alice noticed the Walkers biscuit box on the shelf. There might still be some of Sarah Evans' treats inside. She lifted the box down and took off the lid. Unfortunately, there were no baked goodies. But there *was* a brown envelope folded in half. And on the outside was one word.

'*Agreement*'.

Chapter 28

ALICE POKED HER HEAD out of the door, looked right and left, then closed the door and went back inside. She was unlikely to have been followed, but after the shooting incident she could not be too careful. She sat at Jeremy's table and opened the envelope. Unfolding a piece of cream parchment paper, she read:

It is agreed that Bill Trevelyan will sell to Wilfred Carberry a section of land, approximately two-thirds of the wooded area between Renton Hall and Barleyland and as marked out in the wood. Cost: £1.00.

The agreement was signed by both Wilfred and Bill and witnessed by Cookie Miller. It was dated 25 July 1972.

There was no mention of the dog sculpture. Alice turned the paper over and double-checked the envelope, but there was nothing else. Two well-off men exchanging a relatively small piece of land in a peppercorn sale. The men had been neighbours and friends, presumably trusting each other. And yet. The wood enlarged the

Renton Hall estate, inevitably increasing its value, and it had been acquired for next to nothing. Why?

There were three people who knew. Wilfred was dead. Bill was … well, grumpy. He would not explain anything. That left Cookie Miller.

Roddy was lounging in a deckchair on *Daisy*'s deck, with a sketchbook on his lap. His floppy straw hat was pushed to the back of his head, leaving his cheeks reddening in the sun.

"My deck is being varnished, so I thought I'd stay here until they've finished."

"I didn't know you had decorating plans?"

"I didn't. It was Stanley and Jen's idea. Jen got a splinter in her foot the last time she visited, so they decided to pay for a new surface. It's a very early Christmas present."

"Aren't you worried that a pristine deck will damage your 'go to hell' attitude?"

Roddy pulled off his hat, exposing grey hairs pasted against his head. His brow furrowed. "Dear girl, you are a terrible cynic." His frown turned to a smile. "But a funny one."

Alice nodded at the sketchbook. "Hard at work I see. Exhibition on track?"

"Yes, I'm pleased to say that it is. And a couple of the pieces are not at all bad."

Alice unlocked the hatch door. "I'm sure there's more than a couple that are very good indeed. I'm looking forward to seeing the show."

Roddy followed Alice into the saloon. He threw his hat onto the sofa arm and sat down beside it. "What are you up to this morning?"

Alice opened up her laptop. "Working out who Cookie Miller is."

"Well that shouldn't take long, there can't be many people with a name like that."

Alice read from the screen. "There's an American baseball player and a South African actress … I don't think I want either of them."

"And what is this Cookie Miller supposed to have done?"

Alice told Roddy about Wilfred and Bill's agreement and how Cookie would be the key to unlocking the mystery of the deal.

"Sounds about right." Roddy twirled a strand of beard. "But how does one find a needle in a haystack?"

"Quite. These are the times when you realise the internet does not solve every problem." Alice opened the box of Indian sweets and offered it to Roddy. "By the way, has your blond man turned up?"

"Sadly not, but I'm not giving up. I'll find him." He ate a pistachio barfi. "That was delicious. I could get used to these."

"If I give you another one, do you think it will help you work out who Cookie Miller is?"

Roddy rested his hands under his chin. "I think it probably would." He took a delicate nip from a second barfi. "Wouldn't it be funny if Cookie made cookies and that's why he or she was called Cookie."

"Roddy, that's genius. I thought Cookie might be short for a proper name, but it must be a nickname." She returned to the screen. "To narrow it down, I just need a Miller who was living around Great Wheaton in 1972."

"And was someone that Wilfred Carberry trusted enough to witness the agreement."

"Yes. But I wonder why he didn't ask George? Eleanor's father would have been in his thirties then and they were all living together at Renton Hall."

"Men of Wilfred's generation still treated their children like kids, even when they were adults. Though that's true of most generations."

"I think you're right. From what Eleanor told me, George never knew about the agreement. And Nick only discovered it by chance. Anyway, back to Mr Miller …"

"Start at Renton Hall. Take out the immediate family and who's left?"

"From the photos I found in the attic, I know that in those days they had household and outdoor staff. Hold on, I've got one here." Alice shuffled through a box of photographs that she planned to present to Eleanor in a scrapbook. "This one is family and staff taken in nineteen sixty-nine. Close enough."

Alice placed a black and white photograph on the coffee table. Two lines of people stared into the camera. "That's Wilfred, George and his wife Mary. Eleanor and Nick." Alice pointed out half of the group. "Then there's Jeremy and that's his wife, Sarah. This man" – Alice tapped a finger on the only unaccounted-for male – "must be the herdsman for the cattle. And that leaves these two ladies." Alice turned over the photo. "On the back it says, 'Joyce and Neve'."

Roddy picked up the photo. "Perhaps a cleaner and a cook. So that could be your Cookie."

"Hmm, let's see if I can find them." Alice tapped keys and searched variations of words and names. "I've got something on a Neve Blackburn. Look, there's a picture."

Roddy leaned over and looked at the screen. "Let me see. Yes, she does look like an older version of the woman in your photo."

"She was cook for Lord Neasdon in the nineteen eighties."

Alice scrutinised the faces in the photo. She rubbed her thumb against her middle finger and looked at Roddy. He threw up his hands. Alice tapped the keyboard and scanned more pages. She looked back at the photo of the Carberry household and back at her screen. And then she knew which one of the group was Cookie Miller.

The old lady peered sideways through the narrow gap between her front door and its frame.

"Am I talking to Cookie Miller?" said Alice.

The woman's grey eyes glared. She closed the door and Alice heard metal sliding across metal followed by a thud, as the end of a chain hit wood. The woman opened the door and Alice stepped inside.

"So, you found me out?" Bitty grey hair hung over the woman's shoulders, but Alice had no difficulty recognising her as the woman from the photo. She brushed her hands over her checked dressing gown. "Excuse my pyjamas, I wasn't expecting visitors this morning."

"I want to ask you about something from many years ago. It concerns Wilfred Carberry and an agreement that you witnessed for him. Have you got time to talk?"

The woman folded her arms and looked at the floor. "Well, I suppose it was going to come out sooner or later." She nodded to the sofa. "Sit yourself down. I'll make us some tea."

Alice waited as Sarah Evans stirred sugar in her tea and set the spoon on a tray.

"So, you're Sarah Miller. Or used to be. And you were nicknamed Cookie because of your talent for baking. Then you became Sarah Evans when you married Jeremy. Did I get that right?"

"That's me, though I haven't heard that nickname in years. Wilfred Carberry came up with it as I used to bake cookies for him. But nobody else used it and after he died, everyone forgot I'd ever been called Cookie."

"How did you know Wilfred?"

"My mother was a cook at the Hall back in the nineteen fifties. In those days the Carberrys did a lot of entertaining. Fancy dinner parties. My mum would go in and cook a big dinner for twelve or sixteen people nearly every weekend."

"And I'm guessing that you went with her?"

"It was better than staying at home on my own, as my dad worked in a pub on Saturday evenings. Besides Mum needed the help. And the Carberrys were good to me."

"And when Wilfred wanted a witness for his agreement, you just happened to be around?"

"Yes." Sarah poured milk into her tea. "My mum had left by then and I'd taken over the cooking. Though they weren't doing so many dinners by that stage. Mr Carberry came into the kitchen one evening and he asked me to witness an agreement between himself and Mr Trevelyan. They both signed the paper, then I did."

"Did you know what you were signing?"

"Oh yes, Mr Carberry explained that the boundary between the Hall and Barleyland had changed. The agreement was confirmation of the new arrangement."

Alice crossed her legs, resting her hands on her knees. "And the dog sculpture? That just marked the boundary did it?"

"Oh no, not the boundary. The dog marked the spot where the body was buried."

"Body?" Alice's foot swung out and caught the table leg, rattling cups in saucers.

"Not that I knew about it at the time, of course. If I had, I would never have signed that agreement." Sarah's eyes narrowed.

"Just a minute, I can't quite get my mind around this." Alice put a hand to her head. "You're saying that those men drew up an agreement about a body buried on one of their properties?"

"That's it exactly. Shocking it was. I never thought the same about Mr Carberry after that."

"Who was it? The person who was buried there."

"Mr Trevelyan's mistress."

"No! What?"

If Alice had struggled to comprehend that Wilfred Carberry's agreement was really about the burial of a real person, that it involved a mistress of Bill Trevelyan's made her head tumble. Two respectable so-called gentlemen, burying a body and then agreeing to cover it up? If that's what their agreement was, it was hardly believable. But Sarah Evans seemed very sure.

"I'm certain. Merry Elders told me and she was working at Barleyland at the time. Big kerfuffle there was in the house. Mrs Trevelyan made a terrible scene one day, then she took the children away for a while. This all happened the week before I signed Mr Carberry's agreement."

"So why did you sign it?"

"I didn't know about Mrs Trevelyan's leaving until later on. I used to meet up with Merry once a fortnight. We both had every other Saturday off, so we'd meet for a drink at The Three Bells. But by the time we next saw each other, it had all happened. Of course, I couldn't tell her about me signing the agreement. And it didn't cross my mind that Mrs Trevelyan going away had anything to do with the agreement anyway."

Sarah felt that she had been tricked into being part of a cover-up, involving the discreet burial of Mr Trevelyan's mistress. Disgusted with Wilfred Carberry's behaviour, she handed in her notice to Mrs Carberry. Wilfred had reminded Sarah that her signature was on the agreement. And that it would be best for her if she forgot all about it and never mentioned it to anyone. But she did tell Jeremy. Then they had agreed to forget about it and neither of them had discussed it again. Until Nick Carberry presented the agreement to Jeremy.

"When George Carberry died," said Sarah. "His will stated that the Carberrys' solicitor hand Nick an envelope containing the agreement. Apparently, Nick's father had received it in the same way from Wilfred. George had opened it, sealed it again and left it with the solicitor for safe keeping, so Nick told Jeremy. The agreement was never required and it remained locked away until George himself passed away and left it to Nick."

Nick was already working on his ideas for a swimming pool when he received the agreement. Discovering that he had more land to play with than he thought, he showed the document to Jeremy. They discussed how the dead conifers could be removed, with the cleared space accommodating a pool and changing rooms.

"Naturally, Jeremy told me. We were worried sick that the whole story would finally come out, including my role as witness. Then suddenly Nick and Jeremy were dead.

"Bill Trevelyan discovered that Nick and Jeremy knew about the agreement and he panicked thinking that the body would be discovered," said Alice. "So he shot them."

Tears gathered in Sarah's eyes. "I'd say so. Other than me, nobody knows about that wretched agreement."

Alice looked over her shoulder. "And you feel safe here by yourself? You don't think Bill will come for you too?"

Sarah shook her fists in the air. "Just let him try. I've got my poker ready for him if he does."

Another dead body, but this one from the past. And Bill Trevelyan was responsible for them all. Now that Alice knew what Wilfred Carberry's agreement really meant, it did provide an explanation for Nick and Jeremy's deaths. But Bill's mistress? How had she ended up buried in a pet cemetery marked by a stone dog? And more importantly, who was she?

Chapter 29

CLAUDIA ROWAN WAS DUNKING a croissant into a mug of milky coffee when Alice arrived at the *Great Wheaton Courier*'s office. Claudia was the paper's arts reporter and Alice had asked her friend if she could search the *Courier*'s database. There was a scanned copy of every weekly edition on the computer, so it was likely there would be something to help identify Bill Trevelyan's mistress. Claudia took Alice into a room at the back of the office and showed her where to start.

Alice did not know the name of the woman buried beneath the stone dog, so she typed the word 'Barleyland' into the search box. Several articles popped up. At one point, the Trevelyans had held open garden sessions at their property to raise money for repairs to the local church. The paper had covered the open days. The garden was found to be 'pleasing' and the vicar had given his thanks for the donations received. But there was no mention of another woman.

Alice tried Bill's name next and a surprising number of articles popped up. Bill had been an enthusiastic cricketer in his younger days and there were reports of his batting prowess and athletic fielding. There were photos of him marching in Remembrance Day parades, dressed in a suit and beret, medals pinned to his jacket. Alice played with other keywords, but she could find no trace of Bill's mysterious mistress. She went back to the main menu, where the paper's sections were listed. Arts, Sport – no. Obituaries – not much good without a name. Towards the bottom of the list was a section entitled 'Missing Persons'.

The *Courier* ran a short Missing Persons column from time to time. Started at the end of 1943, it was a service for people looking for loved ones missing during the war years. The column had proved effective and was continued after the War. Alice typed in the date of Wilfred and Bill's agreement, figuring that the woman must have been buried around the same time.

The computer found a number of entries and Alice read messages asking – pleading – for information about family and friends with whom local people had lost contact. Alice pictured distraught parents, siblings, children composing messages they hoped would finally bring home someone special and relieve their agony.

Alice's eyes filled with tears. She walked around the room until she could push emotion to the back of her mind. She sat down again and clicked onto the next page. A message halfway down caught her eye:

MIRIAM GONZALES

5' 1", dark hair, Mexican. Last heard of living with Mrs Dorling in Great Wheaton, but has not been in contact since February 1972. Concerned for her welfare.

A woman, perhaps alone in a foreign country and lodging with a local family. But crucially, Miriam had stopped contacting her sister a few months before Wilfred and Bill's agreement. Could this be the mysterious woman?

"How are you getting on?" Claudia peered around the door.

"Really well, I think I may have found the right person. Now I just need to find an address."

"Oh that shouldn't be difficult." Claudia pulled the laptop towards her. "Call out the information you have and we'll see what we get."

Claudia tapped some keys, then swung the screen back to Alice. "Easy. There's your house, picture and all. Freaky, isn't it?" She perched on the desk. "And what's inside? A body under the floorboards?"

"You may be closer than you think." Alice smiled at her friend. "Thanks, that was a great help."

"Good luck. And if there's a good story in this, don't forget who gave you the address."

No. 27 Poplar Street lay in the shadow of a poplar tree. Alice stepped into a narrow hallway, the peeling wallpaper contributing to its gloominess. But Susan Dorling's smile was as warm as the sun that streamed through the living room window. She urged Alice into a chair in the corner and turned on a standard lamp.

"There's a bit of light on the subject." Susan showed Alice a photograph of her mother. "Mum moved here when she and Dad married in nineteen sixty-four. That was Mum in the garden that year. She was beautiful and such a kind person. I do miss her." Susan looked over

Alice's shoulder. "Anyway, Mum started taking in lodgers after Dad died four years later. Me and my brother were only young, but I remember all our guests, as Mum called them. Including Miriam."

"When did Miriam arrive?"

Susan flicked a long blond plait over her shoulder. "It was January nineteen seventy-one or two. Two, I think. She'd been living in London. She'd come to England with her sister and the pair of them worked in a restaurant. Shepherd's Bush, as far as I remember."

"And the sister stayed on in London?"

"Yes. Miriam said that a friend of hers suggested she move here so the two of them could be closer. Of course Mum knew she meant a man, though Miriam never let on who it was. Anyway, she worked at a French restaurant on the river near The Shipwreck. It's gone now."

"So Miriam worked, got to see more of her friend, and stayed here. And then she disappeared."

"Exactly. Just didn't come home one day. Mum called the police and they searched for her, but they couldn't find a trace of her. She completely disappeared."

Alice held out her hands. "But you told me on the phone that you knew what happened to Miriam."

"Mum had a good friend called Whitey Bale. I thought he was a bit strange, but Mum liked him a lot. Whitey was an eco-warrior long before it became fashionable. He lived in the woods beside the Narebridge Road, fished in the river and foraged for plants and herbs." Susan pushed her sweat-shirt sleeves up to her elbows. "One day, he was looking for rabbits in the woods between Barleyland and Renton Hall, when he heard Wilfred Carberry and Bill Trevelyan talking. He didn't want them to see him, so he hid."

"You mean Whitey was poaching and he didn't want to get caught?"

"Exactly. And Whitey listened. Bill Trevelyan explained that he and Miriam – so Mum was right that they were an item – had argued. He had pushed her, she had fallen and hit her head against one of the headstones in the pet cemetery."

"And she had died. So Bill *had* killed her?"

"Yes, though it sounds as if it was an accident."

"And they buried her in the cemetery, putting the dog there as a marker," Alice said.

"They marked her grave with a dog?" Susan coughed and slapped her chest. "Sorry. Tea went down the wrong way."

"A stone dog. Like a garden ornament."

"You're joking ... Poor Miriam, what a horrible end. And she was such a sweet lady." Susan wiped her cheeks with a tissue. "I'm glad Mum didn't know about the dog bit. She'd have been even more upset, knowing that Miriam had been shoved under an animal like that."

Alice was not sure that Susan had fully understood that the dog was not real, but she decided to leave further explanation. Having got all the information Susan had to give, Alice walked onto the high street and towards the police station.

Nathan Salisbury beckoned Alice into his office as he was finishing a tuna and sweetcorn sandwich. He wiped his hands and opened a thin folder on his desk.

"Thanks for calling yesterday, Alice. Luckily it was not too late to send a forensics team up to the woods and they did recover a body last night. It was buried exactly where you said it was."

"Where the dog sculpture had been?"

"That's right."

Alice told Nathan about her conversation with Susan Dorling and her account of how Miriam had met her end.

"We'll have to try and find this Whitey Bale, to confirm what he heard. Though it was a long time ago. I'm not sure that even the most determined eco-warrior could last that long around here."

"And now that you've got a name, you can formally identify the body."

"That's really helpful, thanks Alice. Show me the missing person ad you found in the *Courier*, would you?" Alice turned on her phone and zoomed in on the photo she had taken of the ad. Nathan read it through, jotting down the details and adding them to his folder.

"If the body does turn out to be Miriam Gonzalez, I'll have to contact her family. I don't suppose her sister is still on that number."

"When will you know for sure that it is Miriam?"

"After the autopsy. Though you've speeded things up by giving a steer on the name. Then we'll be able to speak to her family. We should be able to confirm it's her within a few days."

"Will that include a confirmation on how she died?"

"I hope so." Nathan pulled out a sheet of paper from his folder. "Though I have a preliminary report from the pathologist at the scene." He handed the paper over.

Alice read the two paragraphs and peered at Nathan over the page. "He's sure about this?"

"Absolutely. Given the type of trauma to the head, there

was only one way it could have been caused. He's certain."

Alice turned the Defender into Barn End Road and pulled up just before the entrance to Barleyland. She killed the engine and looked at the wood that separated the Trevelyan estate from Renton Hall. It would have been about this spot that Whitey Bale had crept amongst the trees looking for dinner. Before his hunt had been interrupted by a gruesome conversation between the two property owners.

For Wilfred Carberry it was a calm discussion over how a lovers' tiff ending in tragedy, had presented an opportunity to extend his own estate and increase its value. For Bill Trevelyan, it was about burying his mistress and his crime against her. The price? A few metres of woodland and one pound.

Alice's opinion of both men nosedived. She had no need to brace herself for the conversation she was about to have at the Trevelyan household. She marched up Barleyland's driveway and knocked on the door.

"Hello dear, how nice of you to pop in again." Elsa broke a smile and pulled the door open. "Come in and I'll put the kettle on."

"Don't bother with tea, Mrs Trevelyan. I won't be staying long. Where's Bill?"

"He's in his study, but—"

"Bill Trevelyan," Alice said to the back of Bill's head when she got to the open door of the study, "I know all about your agreement with Wilfred Carberry."

Bill spun around. "What agreement?"

Alice pulled a piece of paper from her jeans pocket. "This one." She gave Bill the paper. "That's just a copy, the police have the original."

"Police?" Elsa clutched the edge of the desk.

"Yes, Mrs Trevelyan. Police."

Red blotches appeared on Bill's cheeks. "Now look here, young lady …"

"Don't you young lady me. You killed two people to keep your sordid secret quiet. And for what? Nick had no intention of touching the pet cemetery. He was going to use the land on the other side of the wood."

"Yes, for now. But what was to stop him having other plans in the future that would involve digging around the cemetery? I couldn't take the chance."

Alice spotted a set of golf clubs beside Bill's desk and she was tempted to wallop him with the driver.

"It's all in the past now, dear." Elsa's soft voice broke the tension. "There's no bringing Nick back."

Alice turned to Mrs Trevelyan. She stepped towards her, towering over the older woman. Alice looked down into her eyes. "But we did bring back Miriam Gonzalez." Elsa's face switched from pink to white. "The police dug her up yesterday."

"I don't know who—"

"Yes you do. You know perfectly well that Miriam was your husband's mistress. You found them together in the woods. Squabbling."

Elsa backed away, but Alice followed her. "You confronted them, didn't you? And they admitted their affair."

"They said they wouldn't see each other again. And I was fine with that."

Alice put her hands on her hips. "You, Elsa, were a long way from fine. In fact you were furious with Miriam. So furious that you went for Bill's rifle and shot her."

Chapter 30

ELEANOR CARBERRY STOOD AT Renton Hall's open door. Wilson, a blue ribbon in his topknot, stood at her feet. Eleanor kissed Alice on both cheeks and shook Joe's hand.

"I'm delighted that you're amongst the first actual guests to stay at the hotel. We're fully booked, so we're doing a special dinner tonight to celebrate. Come in and let me show you Gina's finishing touches."

Gina had already given Alice a room-by-room tour. But there were some small final decisions that had not been made and Alice was keen to see how they had turned out. The estate plans hung just inside the front door. They were surrounded by photos that Alice had found in the attic, of the Carberry family and the staff and pets over the years.

"I was thinking of putting the inventory you did in a glass case here in the corner," said Eleanor. "What do you think?"

"Open at a random page for people to read, I assume?"

"Yes, we can turn the pages every now and again. As there's only a fraction of our collection on display – it will show our guests the other pieces we have."

"That's a lovely idea."

In the bright and welcoming reception area, a young man with a blue streak in his hair and wearing a tweed jacket, took Alice's bag.

"Jeff." Eleanor clutched the man's arm. "This is Alice Haydon and her partner Joe Buchanan. They are my very special guests this weekend, so please take good care of them."

"My absolute pleasure. Please don't hesitate to contact me if you need anything at all. Would you like a drink?"

"I'll take a Guinness." Joe followed Jeff to the bar.

Eleanor and Alice wandered into the library. Logs crackled beneath lustrous flames in an arch-shaped fireplace. "When Gina suggested replacing the fireplace with this modern, rather streamlined structure," said Eleanor, "I was dead against it. But it works perfectly in this room."

"It does. But it's the painting I wanted to see." Alice was looking up at the piece above the fire, and a very large smile spread across her face. She pulled her fingers into a fist and pumped the air. "That, if I'm not mistaken, is the Margaret Thomas painting I found in the abandoned pile in the attic."

"It is. The painting Gina hung there was awful, frankly. I couldn't let it stay. Then I remembered I had this lovely piece. Tom hated it, so we never hung it. As I thought I wouldn't find the right spot for it I was going to give it away. Thank goodness you rescued it."

"It's a great choice for that space and this room." Alice snapped a photo of the painting on her phone. "I thought you'd dumped it because Simon Newgate gave it to you."

Eleanor's cheeks flushed. "I was wrong about Simon on so many levels. I jumped to the conclusion that he was fiddling money from the agency, when actually he was just protecting Nick. When I thought about it, I realised that Simon had always looked out for Nick. Why I ever thought anything else, I really don't know."

Alice remembered the Jamaican invoices that Harry had mentioned. He too thought that Simon was on the take. Did Harry realise that the whole episode was not about Nick fiddling his own company, but Nick covering up for Cheryl? She asked Eleanor.

"Cheryl pestered Nick into lending her money for her failing business. As Nick was at work at the time, he had used the company's account to transfer funds to Cheryl. The auditors were due in the next day, so Simon had knocked up a fake invoice to cover the missing money and the gap in the bank account. He had put everything back to normal once the accountants left."

"So how come you didn't know that at the time. I thought Nick had told you?"

"He did tell me. But I was bathing Wilson at the time and only half-listening. I wrongly believed that Simon had tried to hoodwink Nick."

The conservatory, with its comfy seats, round white metal tables and profusion of plants, was the loveliest of the downstairs rooms. Vibrant yet relaxing, airy yet warming. The morning mist brushed the lake's surface and crept over the fields, but it would lift by lunchtime. Alice imagined herself spending the afternoon watching ducks and squirrels scurrying about their business, perhaps joined by a muntjac deer.

"I want to show you the trees we planted." Eleanor led Alice around to the side of the house. "Back in the day, this used to be a proper kitchen garden. Chef's going to build it up again, so we'll eventually produce all our own vegetables and herbs."

The beds looked empty, most of the activity beneath the soil at this time of year. On the far side ripened apples, like rubies, glowed amongst the leaves.

"Here." Eleanor pointed at four saplings, encased in light mesh, at the east edge of the garden. "They're cherry trees, Nick's favourite. They were his favourite fruit and he loved the blossom." Eleanor leant close to Alice and whispered, "Nick's buried underneath, but don't tell anyone. He would have wanted to stay at the Hall."

Alice brushed down her new green dress as she took Joe's hand at the bottom of the staircase. They headed for the bar. Joe reached for his wallet and took out a note.

"Lucky I keep an emergency cash supply in the kitchen, the bank's cash machine was broken."

In the nick of time! Alice had remembered to replace the money she'd secretly borrowed from Joe's emergency supply, just the day before. Alice winked at him. "Lucky for you, Eleanor said the weekend was on her. And that's on top of my fee. So she came seriously good in the end."

Christian and Devi were in the library. Christian, hair quiffed, clothes styled and a smile as glowing as the fire behind him, hugged his sister.

"The hotel is incredible! We've inspected every room and I love everything about it." He put an arm around Alice's shoulder. "But the artworks, Ally, are awesome. You've picked some great pieces and displayed them beautifully. You must be delighted with what you've done here."

"I am. And despite all the difficulties, this job has been the most rewarding I've had."

Devi kissed Alice on both cheeks. "And what difficulties they were. Dear Nick and Jeremy, victims of a pair of horrible people."

"The Trevelyans were truly the neighbours from hell," said Alice. "While I can't forgive Bill Trevelyan for what he did, I can at least understand that he was protecting his wife. If Miriam Gonzalez's body had been found, Elsa would have been convicted of her murder. But Wilfred Carberry? He covered the whole thing up for a piece of land. Unbelievable."

Joe brought over a tray of cut crystal glasses, each with a measure of amber, which he put down on a round, leather-topped table by the fire. "Jeff gave me these. It's a special sixteen-year-old Irish malt that George Carberry bought in nineteen eighty-one. It should be mature by now."

Christian handed the glasses around, an apple juice for Devi. "Alice, you didn't tell us about the drinks collection. I've seen the wine list, which is fantastic, and they all come from the Hall's own cellar."

"I didn't know there was a basement, so I've never been in it. Thank goodness, as who knows what other secrets are lurking down there."

"Renton Hall's secrets are now uncovered. I'm sure there aren't any more," said Joe.

"Well, the Trevelyans are spending their nights at Her Majesty's pleasure," said Alice. "I'm so pleased that with Bill's conviction for Nick and Jeremy's murders, Eleanor got the quick resolution she wanted. And Nathan Salisbury managed to get in touch with Miriam's family. They're taking her remains to Mexico, so they can lay her to rest in her home town."

"I'm glad that Miriam will be back with her family." Devi took Alice's hand. "And I'm so happy that you invited Christian to share this evening with you. Families are important."

Alice looked into the flames. When her father disappeared one day, never to be heard from again, she had wondered why people made such a fuss about families. Fathers abandoned their children, husbands have affairs, grandfathers lie. What was there to cherish? But in the last few weeks, when she and Christian had quarrelled, the invisible cord that held the two of them together tugged at her heart. She knew that she never wanted to lose her brother again.

She felt a squeeze at her elbow. Joe was frowning. "Are you okay?"

"I'm very okay and I'm so pleased that we are all here together tonight. I want to make a toast." Alice held up her glass. "To you. Christian, Joe and Devi. To my family."

"To families." The four clinked their glasses.

Alice turned to the Margaret Thomas painting above the fireplace. "And to getting one over on Gina Salvini!"

IF YOU ENJOYED SCULPT a Murder, please consider writing a review and let other cozy mystery fans know what you thought. Review on Amazon at: www.amazon.co.uk

Alice Haydon's adventures will continue in the third book of the Alice Haydon Mystery series, available in early 2020.

Follow Lily Ashton at www.lilyashton.com

Printed in Great Britain
by Amazon

35007159R00147